FRESH DIRT FROM THE GRAVE

First published by Charco Press 2023
Charco Press Ltd., Office 59, 44-46 Morningside Road, Edinburgh
EH10 4BF

A CIP catalogue record for this book is available
from the British Library.

ISBN: 9781913867515
e-book: 9781913867522

www.charcopress.com

Edited by Fionn Petch
Cover designed by Pablo Font
Typeset by Laura Jones
Proofread by Fiona Mackintosh

Giovanna Rivero

FRESH DIRT FROM THE GRAVE

Translated by
Isabel Adey

CHARCO PRESS

For Pablo, my younger brother,
who consumed his own shadow.

CONTENTS

Blessed Are the Meek.. 1

Fish, Turtle, Vulture... 21

It Looks Human When It Rains............................. 43

Socorro 69

Donkey Skin... 95

Kindred Deer..137

BLESSED ARE THE MEEK

I

'*W*as it warm, this sticky liquid you found down there?'

'Warm?'

'Yes, warm. Sticky. Was it like an egg white? The white of an egg, Elise, when you've just cracked the shell…'

'I think so, yes. I don't know. I thought it was monthly blood.'

'And yet it wasn't. It was the seed of a man.'

'Yes, Pastor Jacob. I'm telling the truth.'

'The truth is always greater than the Lord's servants. Especially if the servant has been led astray, if she has failed to take the care He demands. We are going to ascertain the truth. In the first testimony we recorded, you said you were in a strange stupor, as though you had surrendered your will to the Devil.'

'I would never surrender my will to the Devil, Pastor Jacob.'

'Don't say "never", Elise. We are weak. You are very weak, it seems.'

'I was asleep, Pastor Jacob.'

'We are taking that into consideration.'

'…Will my father be attending the meeting of the ministers?'

1

'No. Brother Walter Lowen cannot participate in the meeting. The ordeal and the disgrace are keeping him very busy as it is. Go now, Elise, tell your mother to bring the sheets from that night, we need to inspect them. Don't let anyone touch them. Everything is impure now, do you understand?'

'Yes, Brother Jacob.'

II

Her father watches her for a few seconds and then glances away, ashamed, Elise thinks, or angry. Or both. He promptly returns to the business that brought them here, to this small town on the fringes of life. This cluster of houses in no way resembles the colony. They are just scattered constructions stubbornly trying to claim a patch of that dirty sky, empty of birds. Two or three ugly red-brick buildings with pokey windows dominate this expanse of mud. Elise looks at her shoes and thinks she should probably take them off, be more careful with them in case her feet keep growing. She's fifteen, true, but she's heard that her grandmother's feet didn't stop growing until she had her first son at age eighteen. Elise has a lot in common with Grandma Anna: those almost transparent eyes and that rounded forehead, as though thinking up solutions or words of praise. When Elise sings, too, the veins at her temples flow blue like subterranean streams. That's singing with love, her father says. Or at least he used to say. Until the last storm, when the world came crashing down on her.

Elise understands smatterings of the Spanish her father uses for his dealings with the Indian. *Tractor*, *luna* and five hundred *pesos* are the words Elise recognises. Although she isn't so sure about that last one. It

2

could also be five hundred *quesos*. Last year when the June storm burst the riverbanks, flooded the irrigation channels and mercilessly swamped the soya plantations, her father Walter Lowen pulled through by scaling up his dairy business. Graciously she pleaded with him to take her along to the market in Santa Cruz to help sell the cheeses. Over five hundred perfectly set rectangles, made with the best milk, brushed by the scant rays of sunlight that filtered through the high windows in the dairy, where the women were tasked with turning out the cheeses from the moulds. That day she'd understood very little, almost nothing, of her father's conversations with the customers. Some of them stared at her brazenly, perhaps trying to come up with some absurd genetic explanation for those unsettling albino eyes, then whispered to each other or smiled right at her. Was she a beautiful girl, Elise? Not exactly, but she could thank the Lord for her defined facial structure, the way her chin nestled up to her bottom lip, slightly fuller than the top – a trait that meant she'd have to be more unassuming, protect herself better, Grandma Anna herself once said.

Protect herself. From the storm that clawed its way through the colony, destroying everything in its wake by sheer force of water and electricity. Protect herself, indeed, from the ways of the Lord! But may Walter Lowen never hear her blaspheme like that.

Truth be told, though, her father probably used the Lord's name in vain too. Elise had walked in on him crying furious tears in the storehouses as he set fire to the blood-stained sheets, which had finally been returned after days of deliberations in the meetings of the elders and ministers. And crying when, in the middle of the night, like lamp thieves stealing the light from other homes, they loaded their most prized possessions onto the buggy: the rusty casket with their savings; the bundles of clothes; the quilt with intricate, satin-stitched tulips so plump they asked to be touched again and again; the albums and cassettes containing the images and voices of their dead. It shouldn't have been her family who had to leave. But they were the ones who left. 'Don't look back,' Walter Lowen told them, and then she rested her head, covered with a simple scarf, on her mother's soft shoulder and focused on the clattering of the buggy's metal wheels as they registered every pothole, every single hollow hacked into the roads by the storm. Her head against her mother's chest scented with whey, onion and vanilla, the desire stronger than her young spirit to leave everything behind and not look back, just as Walter Lowen demanded, repeating the same refrain, 'Don't look back,' over and over, until his words ceased to make sense because another town with its modern temptations had started to loom on what could only be the horizon.

III

'While the Devil was in you, Elise, did he say anything? Did he whisper things in your ear? The Devil whispers. His voice mustn't have sounded very commanding, I suppose? The Devil seduces, you see.'

'The Devil seduced me, Pastor Jacob? I thought it was Brother Joshua Klassen. I'm pretty sure those were his eyes and that was his birthmark by his mouth, like a grain of rice… I thought…'

'So many details, Elise! I notice you say you're "pretty sure". But the Devil plays these tricks in the imagination when the imagination rebels, and it also makes us submit to observance, to the fear of God. Your parents, Elise, what were they doing? We've heard that Brother Walter Lowen was trying to

4

sign some contracts with a supermarket over in Santa Cruz. If he had shared those tasks out among the community, he would have been able to fulfil all his duties. His hunger for possessions has corroded his self-control. Your parents have neglected your upbringing, Elise. They've failed to maintain order under their own roof; they, too, are responsible for this episode of evil. You are a victim of the world's temptations, and that is why the ministers and I have pleaded with the Lord for mercy. Mercy for you, young Elise, and mercy for your parents and siblings, who are so very ashamed.'

'What will happen to us, Pastor Jacob?'

'This situation calls for much withdrawal, Elise. It is important to look inwards, to matters of the home. For a while you will not work on the farm or in your father's dairy. You can spend your time perfecting other virtues instead. The council is going to do some business with the people of Urubichá. They weave colourful hammocks, but they have no talent for flowers or depictions of nature, which always make the best decorations. You can weave or embroider pieces like those, Elise, humble and harmonious patterns that will please the Lord. All from the comfort of the cabin. You're going to have to look after that fruit you're carrying now, aren't you?'

'This... fruit?'

'It's yours, Elise. If the Lord has allowed its heart to beat in your young womb, you must give thanks. It is the fruit of your body.'

'But... Isn't it the fruit of the Devil, Pastor Jacob? Isn't it the fruit of that seduction, like you say?'

IV

The plot of land they moved to is on the edge of that small town. They didn't have to build cabins on arrival, because the Welkel clan had deserted before them and gave them shelter while they built their own homes. The right hand helping the left. No one has forbidden them to say, 'We've deserted'; there is no need to lie. Elise still misses the brilliant light of Manitoba, but the glare of this astonished sun won't let them hide a single secret either. This isn't just another exodus, it's an escape. They're starting a new story. One day they'll say: Mateo Welkel assisted Walter Lowen with the process of securing credit and purchasing a tractor. That was the genesis of it all. Before the storm, after the storm. And then the tractor.

Three months ago, the families set up a joint venture, hiring out machinery and their own labour for the construction works cropping up around the area. It's amazing how that tractor with its fantastic rubber tyres can lift such vast amounts of material. There's something affecting about the insistent force of the tractor dragging the debris back and forth, like an animal. It's a real Goliath! When the contracts are concluded and the animal is sleeping it off, the fifteen Welkel children, excluding Leah, rush up onto that high throne of commands and levers. Leah watches them from the ground and bids her brothers farewell, waving wildly and giving them infinite blessings, as if at any moment the tractor might take flight to some part of the universe where only men go.

'Over here, Leah,' Elise calls out to her.

Elise decides to let Leah weave her auburn hair into a pretty tangle of braids.

'Where did you get this hair, Elise?' Leah asks again and again, as if Elise hadn't already told her countless times that she's a modern-day mirror image of Grandma Anna, and that women in the Canadian clan are born with locks of hair so red it's almost purple. But patience is required with Leah Welkel, because she's always had problems keeping track of all the things that can happen

6

in a day. She's just one of those people, like the eldest and seventh-born of the Welkel brood, who are also incapable of amassing reality in their heads. God intended them poor and small in every way. That was the price you paid for staying in the same colony for so long, generation after generation. Eventually you marry your cousin, accept that part of your harvest will be spoiled, give up on perfection.

Leah has been possessed in her sleep too, and she's told Elise that the same thing also happened to two of her brothers. Their father ordered them not to talk about it, to cleanse the wound with silence.

'But I don't know how to do as I'm told,' Leah said to Elise, her watery sky-blue eyes full of guilt.

Elise feels no more pity for Leah's innocent stupidity than she does for herself. Self-pity is one of the ways that pride, the greatest of all sins, slips through the cracks in the soul, Pastor Jacob said in one of his sermons, but Elise just can't help it. There must be compassion for her somewhere. Pastor Jacob hasn't been possessed in his sleep. Pastor Jacob isn't going to be alone for the rest of his life, this long life, because his wife left him with a long line of descendants. Elise, on the other hand, will have to look after her parents until the end, especially since the Lord has reaped the crop of her mother's belly and she, Elise, is the last Lowen from the Manitoba colony.

'You won't have a husband, that is true,' Pastor Jacob told her during her first testimony, squeezing her shoulders, 'but you will have a child, a fruit of your own.'

Poor Elise felt her little nipples twitch when Pastor Jacob sentenced her to that punishment. She watched the birds, saw only pride and beauty in their soaring flight. She looked at the cows, their lazy, merciful eyes, and she felt better. If it weren't a sin, if everything weren't a sin, she would have sat down to moo right there in the middle of the farm. Yes, because although she did not know it right then, of all the creatures, it was the cows Elise was going to miss with her heart turned into a beetle. Not those soulless nightingales or those colossal trees, belly swollen like a pregnant animal.

V

'Elise, we were wrong. You are not the only girl who has been violated during the night.'

'No?'

'There are many more, Elise. Many. This is a terrible abomination.'

'And what are you going to do to seek justice?'

'We must gather our strength, Elise. The council of elders will fast. The mothers will fast.'

'What about after the fast, Pastor Jacob?'

'Fasting will give us light, Elise. Do not let despair get the better of you. The Devil preys on such troubles.'

'But the council already know it wasn't the Devil, don't they, Pastor Jacob? In my case it was Brother Klassen. If not, then why did they lock him up, Pastor Jacob? Margareta, Katarina, Aganetha and Lorrae all accuse Dick Fuster.'

'The Devil takes control of our will, Elise, my child. Didn't your parents teach you that? Didn't I myself warn you, in my sermons, about the Devil's snares? Brother Klassen has fallen, just like you, just like Katarina, Aganetha and Brother Fuster. We have all neglected our duties.'

'But Pastor Jacob…'

'Yes, Elise.'

'You are going to punish them, aren't you?'

'They will have to do much penance, yes. They will have to

do a lot of work for the community, a great deal more than the other men…'

'But you are going to punish them, surely? Penance isn't a punishment, Pastor Jacob.'

'These intellectual disputes in your young mind are futile, Elise. From now on I will talk to your father and him alone. We already have all the statements we need. Your words, we already have them. You and the other victims were asleep. The Lord blessed you with that deep sleep so there would be no trauma, so that you and the others would be able to forgive without difficulty. This tragedy hurts all of us as much as you, Elise.'

'As much as me, Pastor Jacob?'

'Off you go now, Miss Lowen. Go home and help your mother.'

VI

This time, with the laws of Manitoba far behind them, Walter Lowen has allowed Elise to accompany him to the site being overseen by an indigenous man; meanwhile the rest of the women stay at home, baking biscuits and turning out cheeses – not so many now – in a room so small it's impossible not to leave smelling of the sweetly bitter scent of the cows.

The Indian and her father have worked all day, taking turns to dig out the soil that spills endlessly from the pit forming in the ground. Elise wanders over occasionally, glances at that narrow tract and feels anxious and dizzy, then adjusts the straw hat on top of her headscarf and sits back down on the construction materials to watch the men. How pale and tall her father looks beside that little man with those blunt features and defiant cheeks, like igneous rocks that the sun might rupture with its harsh rays. She finds it hard to believe, now, that her father cried in the phone booth while dialling the number of Grandma Anna in Canada. 'You have to do something,' she heard old Anna say. And so at dawn, they simply piled their belongings onto the buggy and didn't look back.

When the pit is a black cylinder, a job well done, the two men drink the lemonade Elise serves them. They smell like animals, like those cows the farmers brought back after mating them, not just once but many times. That's what hard work does, it draws out any trace of animal that the Lord has allowed to remain in us, and it cleanses it too. Elise feels queasy and asks her father if she can go home. She knows this is a stupid question, that she's not going to be allowed to wander off on her own in this world of sludge they've moved to; but life itself has changed for them, they can't deny it, and maybe now Walter Lowen will decide that the important thing is to survive, to be together, perhaps even to forgive her.

But Walter Lowen tells Elise she has to stay. He and the Indian are waiting for a third party to arrive, and she must stay there until the end, until the day is over. That was what she wanted, wasn't it? Isn't this what you long for, Elise? To nobly take the place of a son? It doesn't matter if you're pregnant, even better if you're having a boy. A little Lowen lad. We're going to need a lot of manpower to make a go of this new life in Santa Cruz, to remain true to God against all odds. And the fact is, incredible though it may seem, God grows weak in the city; He gets startled, withdraws into the murkiness of deeds.

Elise sits up, smooths down the dress with giant flowers on it, and buries her nose in the fringes of the headscarf that covers her hazelnut, almost purple head and coils around her neck; overcoming the queasy feeling, she instinctively strokes the growth that was planted inside of her in a deep state of unconsciousness, like a bastard annunciation.

The Indian takes a fleeting look at her belly and then seems to forget all about it, distracted by the brief parade of schoolgirls leaving or escaping from their classrooms at this time of the day, exultant and full of chatter. For a while Elise, too, forgets about the living lump eating away at her youth from inside of her, where no one had been until that night, after the storm. She looks at the girls in their blue and white uniforms, and their laughter feels like golden needles sewing invisible patterns in the air, floating above the music that plays from their phones, a music that is a furious, cheerful vibration. She looks at their trainers, their bronzed calves, those short bobs and those high cheekbones, where there are no freckles, only a flush of pink and an unfamiliar intensity. And in contemplating the scene, she knows she is absurd and alone.

Walter Lowen, though, doesn't get distracted. He's still a young man, and he's used to swift transactions and keeping his books in order. All the same, Elise senses an uneasiness about her father, something distinctly nervous in his brusque mannerisms. Of all the words she's been picking up in Spanish, not one enlightens her to the meaning of the conversation these two men are having. She's not to know that, in a way, talk has now turned to politics.

'You're not afraid that the press might come? Those journalists are real nosy,' says the Indian. His mouth is clamped around the little balls of coca leaves he's always chewing and keeps in a plastic bag. He smells like those leaves too. Ever since she's had that lump inside of her, wriggling with glee and splitting her adolescent hips, everything has been smell for Elise. But the scent of this man, of his dark mouth squeezing the sap from the leaves, is one she likes. He smells of forest. A dirty, deep forest.

'That, too, is why we deserted' Walter Lowen explains. 'It's a disgrace,' he says, shaking his head to fend off the invisible crows of his memories.

'In your religion it's forbidden to kill, right?' says the Indian, almost smiling, his strong teeth stained the colour of that bitter forest.

'That power is God's and His alone – that's what they say, that's what we all learn,' says Walter Lowen.

The Indian is tickled by the Mennonite's strong eastern accent, his words snipped short by the excess of oxygen in his breath. *What would Walter Lowen be like if he'd taken his family to live in the mountains? In El Alto, for example. There, no one would have got off scot-free. The men would have stood up full of courage, hungry as wolves, and the women, even worse, make no mistake. Petrol, kerosene, alcohol, sticks, dynamite, stones; they'd grab anything they could to bring justice. And the culprit – oh, the culprit! – would be made a mighty torch of redemption, crying out for mercy until his throat burst while the bystanders spat out his crime at him. But these camba Mennonites have too much faith. At most they leave, like this Walter Lowen guy, who claims he 'deserted' like some soldier from the Chaco War. But Pachamama doesn't just bury the past like that. Not even for these camba Germans, or wherever it is they come from – that's no way to move on from the damage done.*

'You know, in the beginning I thought you'd deserted because of the government. Folks can't keep so much land all for themselves these days, not even a large group like the Mennonites,' the Indian says. 'They've taken land off people in Paraguay too. In the old days, of course, you gringos from the sects came here at the government's invitation. Our National Revolutionary Movement was the most welcoming of all, you know. With his agrarian reform of '52, old Víctor Paz Estenssoro doled out land as if he were handing out glasses of chicha or singani. "Here, for you," to the Japanese; "here, for you," to the Mennonites. "Workers to the mines, peasants sow your seeds," said he. But of course, that land was pure wilderness, wasn't it? You people had to work real hard at the soil, overcome the rainforest, forge paths, build your own houses, true? If you really think about it, though, Mr Lowen, everything happens for a reason, wouldn't you say? What happened to your daughter forced you to get out of there quick, like a soul carried away by the Devil himself.' The Indian snorts at his wry remark, pleased with this cultural wisdom, which springs from some place more profound than his own nature.

'It was a tragedy…'

'Forgive me, Mr Lowen, but it's the truth. You left your beloved Manitoba just before the government showed up to parcel off those plots of land. It must be real nice, that land. You deserted at just the right time, Mr Lowen. Welcome to this neck of the woods, Mr Lowen,' he laughs, stuffing his mouth with another ball of the wonderful green gold that brings out such a strong desire in Elise. Oh, to be a cow and to graze, delirious with happiness, on the soft green pastures.

VII

'You will be mine, Elise Lowen. Whenever I want you. Like right now. Tonight you're my bitch. I'll get inside of you when it's dark, I'll be in your dreams. I'll keep coming back, and I'll take your breath with me. How warm your breath is. And the taste of your neck.'

'Elise, Elise, get up, Elise.'

13

'Mother?'

'What were you dreaming, Elise? Don't dream like that anymore, my girl. Forget, forget.'

'Mother…'

'We're leaving, Elise. Help me. Gather our clothes. Put the shoes in a box.'

'Leaving? Where are we going?'

'Far away, Elise. To Santa Cruz. You're going to give birth there.'

VIII

'That's him,' says Walter Lowen, pointing his pale chin at the man in blue dungarees walking towards them. The Indian takes another ball of coca leaves; Elise wishes she could stuff something into her mouth too, a whole forest, leaves and flowers, thorns and all, to calm herself down, but also to calm the growth that has started taking its aggressions out on her pelvis and beating her stubbornly, as if her young body weren't enough of a home for anyone, like a suffocation growing inside and outside of her. The fact is, Elise has recognised the man from the storm. Or rather, she hasn't exactly recognised him – it's not as if she should, there's no way she could – but the rice-like birthmark by his mouth is like one of those dots that join together to form a picture. Her fear does the rest, filling in the features of that face so close to her own. She can't trust her memories, and yet still she feels the stinger splitting her chest open and a black gale rushing through her, tearing her like a length of cloth, from end to end, with no chance of being stitched together again. She remembers that she was sleeping, tired from carting the moulds of cheese from the dairy to the dining room

14

because the river, wrenched from its banks by the storm, was forging ahead like a demon, a monster that was splitting into a thousand watery tentacles and seeping into the storehouses. The cabins were safe because they were held up by strong, sturdy stakes that had been anchored onto the hills by the men in the community, each helping the other. She was sleeping, yes, when that foul smell, that mixture of poison, detergent and sweat, assaulted her like fumes, like the sulphurous scent that Pastor Jacob says the Devil oozes when he passes by.

Do you like that, Elise? Had you done it before? Not even in your dreams, right?

Walter Lowen had to accept that his little girl, a virgin, had been the enemy's chosen one. It was a test for everyone. At first Elise Lowen did not deny, did not correct, did not share his suspicions. Then she was confronted by the vision of Joshua Klassen spraying her with the concoction he used to put the cattle to sleep in order to castrate them, heal their hooves or pull dead calves out of them. It was him, Elise said then. But by that point, the rumour that the Devil had made Manitoba its temporary realm had become an immense truth, just as the crescent moon of that girl's little bump was true.

Had you done it before?

But there Joshua Klassen is again. There, like an olfactory ghost, the dreadful vapour trail of the narcotic spray that crushed the dignity of the Lowen cabin forever that night.

You will be mine. I'll get inside your nights, your body, your neck. Always. I'll get inside, Elise. And he takes her young hand and wraps it around his swollen penis, forcing her to realise, even in this vile unconsciousness, that this is the asp where the Devil brews his own. *You smell of calf, Elise. I like that. And I like when you cry, Elise, it really turns me on. Go on, cry into my ear, little calf.*

No, it's not her consciousness that makes Elise recall Joshua Klassen lifting up her nightdress, taking off her linen panties, drooling on her tight vulva, climbing on top of her the same way she herself, oh the horror!, had seen him mounting the Welkels' cow, that poor creature she secretly called 'Carolina' like the one in the Canadian short story Grandma Anna had read to her, warning her that it was wrong to give animals names because the Lord had put them on the face of the earth to be dominated by man. And yes, Joshua Klassen had dominated Carolina in the same lustful, revolting way that he had violated Elise in her sulphurous dream. *I will get inside of you, like I've been inside of Carolina. You're going to moo in my ear, Elise Lowen.*

So of course, she does not understand why her father, Walter Lowen, is forcing her to stay. Perhaps he's hoping she'll ask for forgiveness for his sin, for the shame, for the desertion? Or to explain that she wasn't the one who fell into terrible temptation, into the revolting trap of spray and drool, and that his whispers repulsed her, even in her unconscious state? Elise doesn't like feeling this way, but the flashback to that horror makes her wish the Indian were her father instead. How much more protected she would have felt then.

Still, Elise clings to what meekness she has left when Walter Lowen runs his hand along her back, gently supporting this little girl's spine, which is giving way, curving under the demands of her growing uterus. She trusts in her father and his love for her. But she also knows him well and understands that he can turn the other cheek without so much as blinking. Like the time a thief snatched his backpack containing six months' earnings and he invited them to dine with him at his own table. Her father paid for the man's journey from Santa Cruz to Manitoba and made sure he had plenty to eat. To prove what? That God had blessed him with the more generous spirit? That he could turn an insult into a friendship? 'It's just money, he didn't steal anything important,' Walter Lowen said that day. This time it's not about money, but still her father is prepared to surrender the cheek that has been bruised again and again. This time it's about her. If anything, Elise thinks, holding back the urge to cry, it's her cheek, it's her belly, her future that has been wronged, spoiled, sullied. Elise looks at her father, bewildered; she wants him to explain why he has summoned Brother Klassen to this absurd meeting. Please, just tell her why.

Oblivious to these ideas fighting like scavenger birds inside Elise's head, Walter Lowen fixes his gaze on Joshua Klassen and welcomes him. In Plattdeutsch, he says:

'How good that you came, Brother Joshua. Today we're going to do some business.'

Joshua Klassen smiles, and he dares to smile at Elise without giving in, for so much as a second, to the urge to look down at that belly where he planted an unwanted seed. Poor Elise, poor Carolina.

The Indian moves closer, too. He holds out his hand to the newcomer. 'So you must be Joshua,' he says, grinning. Elise begins to sympathise with that smile, starts to understand it. The mud, those horrible red brick buildings and that cityscape of yellowish trees no longer seem so ugly to her. There's something this man can do for her, for the Lowens, Elise senses.

'Here's the deal,' the Indian starts to say, inviting the Mennonites to move closer to the freshly dug pit of earth. 'You will not prosper, will not build even a humble shack, unless you ask for forgiveness.'

'Forgiveness?' Joshua Klassen arches his brows. 'Whose forgiveness?' He glares, red-faced, at his fellow Mennonite, the deserter he perhaps shouldn't have agreed to meet, a man the whole colony has disowned for running from his fate. What a coward, that son of God!

'Pachamama, who else? It's no good just asking her for solid foundations, right? You've got to offer her something in return, some fruit, a llama's foetus, some candy, something!' The Indian chuckles, convulsing with happiness. Elise wants to feel that again: the giddiness, her lungs about to explode because this whole life is too dazzling to bear in all its glory.

Joshua Klassen is infected by the man's extraordinary laughter. Elise sees him shaking in that borrowed laughter, getting inebriated on something – an unwarranted sense of well-being, she supposes – and teetering from side to side in that huge body her father was incapable of facing up to, those hairy hands, *any trace of animal that the Lord has allowed to remain in us*. Elise hates him. Perhaps that's why she fails to notice the hint of glee that sparks when the events unfurl, perfect in their violence, sudden and beautiful in their simplicity: the Indian, still laughing, pushes Joshua Klassen into the deep, deep pit, while Walter Lowen, abandoning his own salvation once again, jumps up onto the tractor and starts to return to the jaws of the earth what they have spent the whole day wresting from it. Heap by heap, the dirt covers Joshua Klassen's cries, irate, incredulous at first, then increasingly weak.

'A sacrifice, that's what it is,' the Indian says, spraying his leaf of mouth-watering resin over that makeshift chullpa. 'You will be at peace, Pachamama,' he seems to be praying. 'A sacrifice, that's what it is,' he says.

Elise does not know what he means by sacrifice, but it's her girlish heart, and not her mind, that needs to understand. That same startled heart which now impels her, like a faithful animal, to outstretch her white, calloused hands and grab fistfuls of dirt, carefully, furiously, breaking her nails. She looks at those fistfuls as if it were the first time she'd encountered the grainy consistency of that substance, then she throws them over the mound of earth like an offering of her own, a small bunch of dirty, precious flowers. For her, for Leah Welkel, and for Carolina. For Carolina, too.

FISH, TURTLE, VULTURE

*Moving the Shadows is used
when you cannot see through
your opponent's mind.*

Miyamoto Musashi

Tell me more, she says, pushing the plate of tortillas towards him as if she were paying him to tell the tale with that warm, fragrant dough.

I've already told you everything, Amador sighs.

You say the two of you drank that blood. You say my son didn't want to drink that blood.

It was all congealed, almost worse than urine, ma'am. He gives a bitter smile.

Either that or drink his own... My poor boy.

Amador lifts a tortilla and divides it carefully, almost with the mysticism of a priest consecrating bread. He can't help but close his eyes for a few seconds while he chews. Ever since he's had something to eat other than the oily fish he used to catch in the hollow of his hands, it's just something he does. Closes his eyes and chews.

And poor you, of course. Only you're still alive, if you understand? But anyway... Tell me, are the tortillas good?

Very good, ma'am. I'm so grateful that you invited me here. I know you wish it was your son sitting in this chair instead of me, telling you about life on the water, about how fierce a shark can get. But he isn't, that's just how it is. I'm here. And you're here, and it's so nice of you to invite me to eat with you, so kind of you to make these tortillas for me... Look, I'm really sorry...

Don't you worry yourself, Amador. My pain is mine alone. It's a mother's grief, you know?

For me, I swear, the hardest thing was dumping the body in the sea. Forgive me for putting it like that, in the raw... But at least I can talk about it these days without bursting into tears like a little kid. I can talk about these things now. It's the therapy. The government's paying for me to go to therapy. The psychologist asks me all these questions, she sits there quietly and waits for me to speak, she asks me about my dreams, and I tell her that the ocean comes back, that it comes back like a giant bird, that my throat starts to close up, like with shoe glue, that I...

When did you dump the body in the sea, Amador? What day was it? Did you pray? At the very least, did you pray? the woman repeats, her eyes damp but not spilling a single tear, as if she held the power to deliver the relief or the penance of crying. It's hard to tell this woman's age, all dressed in black like that. Elías Coronado was only young, and he said his mother was getting on in years when she had him, that she thought of him as a miracle.

Amador wants to leave. But he wants to keep chewing. Those tortillas, and food in general, remind him he's alive. Still, he really ought to leave. For the past week he's been staying in a guesthouse in the fishing village just to keep the promise he made to Coronado during those long conversations on the boat. It was good to talk to the dead guy. You could talk to that chero about anything. Amador knows now that his crewmate was only fifteen years old, but when he signed up to the fishing cooperative he told them he was eighteen. He was well read, young Coronado, he always had something interesting to say. About Islamic State, about Japanese legends from centuries gone by, about flesh-eating bacteria and bird migration. Shame he'd never thought of looking into ways of surviving a shipwreck. He definitely missed a trick there. If you're going to fill your head with all that knowledge, at least learn how to fight the dogs for scraps if it comes to it.

In the guesthouse, Amador has been sleeping with the windows closed. He doesn't want to hear the harbour swell. That hissing of snakes slips into his ears and gives him terrible nightmares. The hunger expanding inside him like a helium balloon, an animal made out of empty space, a blind animal that scorches his guts and fills him with misery. The sun caving in on him with all its wickedness.

But in two days he'll be leaving. Not for home, where he came from; there's no way he's going back to El Salvador. That shit's still too tough. No, he's bought a little house in the quietest part of Michoacán, in the mountains, where the wind dominates the sun and it's always raining. If there must be water, let it be from above, simple. The real reason he's come to Coronado's mother's house in this dirty part of the Costa Azul is to give her a cheque, half the fee he received from the famous journalist who's going to write his story. It's Elías's story too, even though he's dead.

Dead.

Amador told himself this again and again as he looked at Coronado's motionless body, not lucid enough to clearly perceive his belly swelling up, no longer from all the hunger and desperate gastric juices but from death, plain and simple. He couldn't say when the boy's face turned so rigid and pale, despite the rays of sun still plummeting down onto his skin.

Is it nice being dead? he asked his crewmate three or so days into his death, which must have been no later than day 98. Like a prisoner, he made a habit of marking the inner wall of the bow each time the moon appeared. He trusted the moon more than the sun, because that light was poisonous and made him see things.

Coronado sat up. His cracked mouth made an effort to smile.

You're a selfish son of a bitch, man, Amador whimpered. He wanted to hug the dead boy or cradle his head in his chest, but Coronado had already sagged back against the damp wood of the boat. The sun didn't bother him. He didn't squint or lift his arm to shield his eyes. He seemed happy.

Amador moved closer to Coronado and shook him gently. The body was light, even when Amador couldn't be bothered using his strength, the little he had left, which he used to slit seabirds' throats to suck, no longer with disgust, on their sticky blood.

Amador lifted his crewmate's t-shirt, the one he'd teased the boy for wearing when they boarded the boat because it betrayed his youth, the touching naivety of a novice declaring to the world his pride at having joined the ranks of the tiburoneros, the shark hunters. The fishing cooperative sold those t-shirts to tourists, but few of the men who worked on the boats actually wore them. Cotton was no good for the sea. Sweat made it heavy, and if a strong breeze was blowing, they'd be sure to catch not a shark but a nasty cold. Coronado had only signed up a little over a month ago and must have thought the t-shirt legitimised him, like a sub in football.

Amador was shocked to see a string of fuzzy hairs climbing to the boy's navel. He was thin and, bloated belly aside, even skeletal now as a result of those interminable days when he refused to eat any more rotten seaweed or the few fish and medium-sized turtles his fellow traveller and shipwrecked sailor hunted down, because hunting was what that was, not fishing: driving his fingernail into the heads of sea turtles that skimmed the boat and biting seabirds' necks before finishing them off with his bare hands. At first he'd used the little knife, but he was afraid he might lose it in that constant battle with the water. They had to keep it safe in case they spied land and had to release the buoys. Coronado was refusing to collaborate. And here he was, turning green as if nothing mattered to him. Though the boy's limp arms no longer resisted, Amador struggled to stretch out the t-shirt that had glued itself to the boy's drenched torso. Lifting him just a touch by the part of the back where the spine begins to narrow, the sensation of doing something lustful, something he might do with a woman, made him shudder.

Amador soaked the t-shirt and tied it around his head. Coronado was well and truly dead, after all; he was hardly going to need it now. Let him shrivel up and dry like an animal, the coward. In days of starvation, an exquisite spread like that was a sight to be seen. A poor fisherman could devour his own hand.

The relief from the wet cloth was short-lived. As the saltwater trickled down from the makeshift turban it stung his dry mouth, made his constricted throat hurt even more. Suddenly a wave of nausea more intense than the sickness he usually felt forced him to lie down along the length of the boat, in the part where the false mast was casting a thin strip of shade. He stretched out beside Coronado. The good thing about being there, lying next to a corpse, was that he didn't feel inhibited. He could watch the boy without interruptions, as if delving into those placid brains, which had been freed of all torment. He even tilted Coronado's face to get a better look at him. The boy couldn't see him because his eyelids were closed, but that was a good thing. Amador would have felt very uncomfortable if, even after turning completely stiff,

the boy continued to watch him with the same excessive curiosity
he'd shown when he was chosen to join him for the expeditions
aboard the Chavela. *The pay was a pittance. Maybe the dead*
boy would come to him now demanding a fair wage, as if it were
up to him. Those jerks at the cooperative always took advantage
of the new recruits. Let them start from the bottom. But from the
bottom of what? When everything was ocean, just watery vomit
with nothing on the horizon, a giant emerald back full of evil
and beauty. It was a miserable place.

You really don't have to pay me anything, Coronado's mother says politely, pushing away the money order Amador has placed between her hands.

Amador is still chewing as he makes for his fourth tortilla. He wants to stop, but the soft, warm taste of that food keeps him there, in that modest dining room. Out back is a little yard with a roof assembled from badly cut sheets of corrugated iron, like quartz claws. Ferns, coloured fungi that resemble foetuses, herbs, graceless flowers and chives populate this woman's kingdom of plants. Amador feels sorry for her.

The woman watches him eat. Amador can't smile at her while he eats. Since returning to land, he usually has lunch and dinner alone, alert to the sounds of his teeth grinding. This isn't something he's ever mentioned in therapy.

The cheque is still there. Amador wonders if it's an insult. He hurries to swallow and says:

It's not my money I'm giving you, ma'am.

Go on, help yourself to a drink. I made it with homegrown herbs. From my little vegetable patch outside.

Amador clutches the glass of linseed juice. He chooses not to dwell on the off-yellow hue of the liquid; it looks too much like the cloudy urine that he and Coronado started to pee two weeks into being lost at sea.

I just want to know about my son; tell me every little thing. Did he suffer terribly in his dying moments? Did you show him compassion?

Compassion?

Amador takes a deep breath and holds the air from his stomach in his mouth, like the therapist told him to any time the panic threatened to tighten his chest. It's a technique Amador has used before, breathing as if diving into a thick black ocean with limited oxygen reserves. Like the time he ventured into the snake-riddled bushland in Garita Palmera, on the run from the Mara Salvatrucha. With his backbone pinned to the trees, he held his breath. He'd rather die like that, of suffocation, poisoned by his own gases, than at the mercy of a long stick to the throat and the guts, tearing his internal organs, boring at the shit people carry inside. Back then he was not to know that panic, like the Devil, appeared in many guises. Right now, for instance, this woman is asking if he showed compassion for Coronado and forcing him to sift through his memory for more precise episodes from those times when the ocean, in its leaden immensity, tossed the boat back and forth, spilling water in and out of Coronado's open mouth. Watching that rocking motion put him in a trance. Coronado throwing up water and salt, little bits of rotten seaweed, but no longer complaining.

Is death nice? he asked him again.

And Coronado replied that yes, death was the best.

Amador snapped: You dare tell me that, but you don't even have the courage to look at the sky, to see how soon it's going to be light. You don't have the slightest fucking clue whether it's going to be a cloudy day or if this rotten sun is going to burn the skin off our backs. And then you smile – of course you smile, insolent ape. I've been watching you, and I know that the left side of your mouth sort of curls up when you find something funny. You can thank your lucky stars that fuck all works around here; if it did, I'd take a photo of you as proof of your bullshit. You don't have the balls to live, asshole.

You're right, the woman says, Elías did do that when he smiled. I used to find it disarming. You know, he couldn't tell a lie either. The second he started lying, his little mouth would curl up at the corner. You're very observant. Take a look at this picture, it's from when he started high school. Do you see him there? He was smiling like that because…

I should probably be getting back to the hotel, Amador interrupts. The house has been piling up towards the back wall; before long it'll fit into the vegetable patch under those sheets of corrugated iron. That's what the late afternoon sun does to houses with low roofs, it shrinks them, winds them up, dragging the shadows of the furniture towards a subtly illuminated spot. Amador, though, is calmed by the closeness of the night. During the day everything is ablaze with light, completely exposed to the fear of eyes.

Please don't leave just yet, Coronado's mother says. You can even get to Chocohuital on foot if you feel like walking.

I've already told you everything, ma'am, Amador pleads. Because in truth that's what his voice is, a *let me go, let me close my eyes and stuff cotton wool into my ears, as if I were a lousy corpse too.*

But the woman is already on her way over with another plate of tortillas. Not so many, just enough to fuel the traumatised lust of this man who dumped her son's body in the sea. He should have brought him back to her, even in mummified form, like meat marinated with lemon juice and burnt to a crisp by the sunlight. He should have brought him to her as machaca, then, as dried meat.

Eat, eat, please. It's good when you're hungry and can satisfy it, no? This was Elías's favourite recipe, I make it without the instant yeast. It has a different flavour, wouldn't you agree?

Amador smiles. He notices that the woman has reverted to niceties to keep him there. Still, he has no desire to make up stories about things that never happened. He'd rather stay schtum. It's your right, the therapist told him, it's your right to chew on your memories as if they were blades of grass. Then he helps himself to a little more linseed juice, drinks it with less haste than before. Judging by the steam rising from the plate, those tortillas must still be piping hot.

What would you like with your empanadas, young admiral? Amador asked Coronado one day, it must have been day 27 at the latest; he can still remember because he'd always been superstitious and had hoped this day would be different, that the sky would remain overcast and free from any great flashes of light so as not to deter the rescue helicopter with the sun's unrelenting rays. Yes, on that lucky day the helicopter would launch itself into low flights and unfurl a net not unlike the ones they used to bundle up sharks like new-born babies. So soft to look at but so aggressive to touch, the skin of those creatures.

So, it was day 27 and he had decided to lift the spirits of the bronzed, disgruntled zombie that his 'admiral' had become – that was how he'd referred to him from the start, in a bid to make the tedium and despair more tolerable. From the water he read out the menu: seaweed pastries, shrimp pastries, tuna or 'takeyourpick' pastries?

Coronado smiled and ordered the impossible: chalupas,

please, lots of salsa! The boy was craving the taste of that crispy fried masa from back home.

And Amador swam with the best technique he could remember from that other sea, a homely sea, the filthy Salvadorean sand, the now forgotten aquatic world in which he'd steeped the years of his childhood, not long before the Mara Salvatrucha set their sights on him, either to recruit him or to mess with him. At that time, the ocean was a haven. And now? Yes, now too, in a way.

What salsa do you want? Avocado or chilli?

Red chilli, captain, the boy played along for a few minutes. That was all he was, just a boy, a child with traces of puberty lingering on his scrawny ribs. The whites of his eyes, stained by the poison he'd unwittingly ingested from the guts of that seabird, confirmed his calling as a corpse. Elías Coronado had been dead from day one, ever since he'd signed up to the fishing cooperative. Maybe it was actually Amador's crewmate who dragged him towards this fate, to the infinite sea of the dead. Maybe Coronado was the hook and Amador had just let himself be led by the mouth to a surprising hellscape, a liquid transfiguration of fire, a truly sick joke.

And here they were, Amador using an imagination he never knew he had, to feed what remained of this tattered wreck of an admiral. He floated a few metres away from the boat, a cautious distance. Truth be told, he didn't have the strength to swim for more than five minutes. He collected anything that moved in the little swells of water the waves formed around his body; he closed his eyes for a moment, no longer just to let his instincts perform the task of hunting, but to imagine that those constant lashings were a form of divine love. God hadn't abandoned him; the simple fact that the boat had not capitulated to the infinite belly of the ocean, despite all the fissures along the seven metres of the deck, was proof of this loving miracle, of this miracle played out in small perpetuities: one day, then another day, then another day.

Amador returned to the boat with fish that he beheaded with a bite to stop them slithering away. He tossed them onto the deck as best he could. At first Coronado showed some curiosity, spurred on by the hunger, but lately he barely touched those nautical tortillas. Increasingly gaunt by the day, his face barely recalled his age. He was an old man on the edge of time. Perhaps that was the very nature of being lost at sea.

Listen, the woman takes a deep breath, summoning courage from her own entrails, where she carried Elías in the final flush of her ovaries, I'm going to ask you something. It's nothing new, those TV presenters and journalists have already asked you every question under the sun; I'm sure you're kind of sick of having to answer like a parrot with no memory. It's just, you know, people are still amazed that you survived out there, alone like a soul abandoned by the Lord, and for more than four hundred days! I can imagine what they must have thought when you showed up on that faraway shore, when you surfaced from the water, staggering around like a drunkard, so they tell me... They must have thought you were some kind of demon. Because I tell you, only demons can overcome all that hunger, fiendish cold and sickness, isn't that right? The rest of us are more human. And I'm sure they've already asked you, Amador, well, you know, how you managed to stay alive for that whole journey. And I suppose each time you explain, it gets easier, right? I suppose it's like praying, huh? We keep asking God for a miracle again and again, even though we know the mercy we seek is impossible. That's what it must be like talking on TV, right? But please, Amador, with me, please speak the truth.

Towards the end of her little speech, the woman's voice starts to sound choked. Amador wants to give her some distraction or distract himself, wants to occupy his mouth with his obsessive chewing. He extends his arm across the Formica table to reach the plate with those two large, deckle-edged tortillas, smooth and golden like medusae in formation. But the woman snatches the plate from him.

Amador looks at her without discernible surprise.

Ask me whatever you want, he says. Now it's his hands, Amador's hands, that resemble creatures from the deep, his fingers outstretched on the Formica with the subtle hope of controlling the slight tremor that strikes at least three times a day.

Day 93, perhaps two or three days before Coronado decided not to open his eyes again and the corners of his mouth began to look more cracked than they should – later, Amador would check his mouth and see that the poor admiral had been nibbling little bits of his own tongue – Amador spotted a long, humble vessel. It was a fishing boat. Judging by the oblique sunrays spilling from the sky, he guessed it must be around five in the afternoon. But then again, he couldn't be certain. He knew the boat was sailing eastwards, but he had no idea whether at that unknown point on the horizon springtime was beginning or ending. In any case, the breeze was already ice-cold and the sparkles on the sea resembled diamonds. Not that Amador had ever seen a diamond.

A boat! Look, a boat! Let's go, don't play dumb with me, wake up! A boat!

Coronado watched impassively. He didn't even bat an eyelid. He'd been that way since the previous afternoon.

Amador grabbed the oar with a piece of cloth dangling from the end, the only thing they could wave as a signal of life and distress in all that horrifying immensity.

Give me a hand, you little shit! he pleaded.

Coronado looked at him with the same cold-hearted, scientific glare as those birds, the ones that had started perching on the bow with a patience that had since turned obsessive. Coronado had told him that they were griffon vultures, but Amador could have bet his oar the boy was making things up because his screws had come loose. Befuddled, that's what he was. Vultures couldn't be that pretty, they weren't as elegant as these birds, which had the graceful necks of seabirds but strong, lethal beaks, like weapons of war.

Amador decided to use the strength he normally rationed in the daytime to hunt turtles or to scale bigger fish if he got lucky, and so he launched himself into the sea with the rope tied to his waist in case he couldn't reach the fishing boat levitating about two miles away. He swam with slow strokes, as if relishing the salty, deadly mantle that was transforming his torso into the primeval back of a reptile. Coronado was shrinking.

The crew must have thought that Coronado was an effigy, one of those traditional fetishes that some fishermen displayed on the bow of their boats to ward off storms. He kicked about for a while and strained his eyes. The clouds had frayed into pathetic tatters. The sun was an unrelenting purge.

The boat looked about ten metres long, not much bigger than the Chavela. On the starboard side were symbols that Amador couldn't understand. A Japanese word? Chinese? Korean? In the days when Coronado still talked, before they got lost at sea, he used to tell him Japanese legends about ghost girls and warriors from centuries past, samurais who recited poetry as they decapitated their enemy; that boy was full of surprises, a truly knowledgeable little fucker. What did he hope to get out of fishing? To pay for a degree? And just look at him now, more silent than Christ himself.

He had a couple of metres still to go, but the fishing boat was floating farther away. Or perhaps he had misjudged the distance? He looked towards the Chavela and could just about make out Coronado. It might be him, the motionless figure outlined there, but then again maybe it was the end of the oar he always kept handy in case he had to take out a turtle with a hefty whack to the shell.

When Amador eventually reached the boat, he stopped for a couple of minutes to catch his breath. He couldn't believe he'd made it all the way.

Hey there! he shouted. His voice was croaky. That was how little he'd used it. Only with Coronado.

Captain! Hello? Anyone there?

The silence was overwhelming, nothing but the dreadful licks of the sea striking the base of that boat, so bloated it looked fit to burst, and a subtle hum, which might also be a figment of his imagination. The night before, Amador dreamt he could hear the whistling of the Mara Salvatrucha, and when he awoke his head was still pounding.

Amador decided to take a risk – what else was a man like him to do with all the desperation he'd accumulated over these months at sea? He hoisted himself onto the gunwale and jumped onto the deck. No one came out to greet him. They might even have mistaken him for a pirate and shot him. But who would shoot a semi-naked man with his beard down to his chest, all riddled with bugs like a troglodyte? A man who could barely manage to keep his balance, who was clinging to his own voice like the last human being in existence. Captain?

Amador? the woman says. Are you going to answer me or not?

The tortillas are right there; they're just warm now, perfect for consoling the palate, the sensation of infinite hunger that perhaps Amador will never overcome.

Of course, ma'am. Please, just ask.

Can you tell me about the hunger you felt? You see, I've never been hungry, not what you'd really call hunger, because I've worked since I was just a little girl.

Of course I understand that going hungry for days can be like having some sort of animal living inside you, right? A tiger, something like that. I sometimes fall asleep thinking about it, about how hungry my Elías must have been, my poor boy. I'm asking you, Amador, please tell me everything, don't be afraid of upsetting me.

That hunger, ma'am, I swear, it's not the kind of thing you can put into words. After we'd eaten something, fish or turtle, I'd tell Coronado — I mean Elías, your son — that we should go straight to sleep. The fact is, falling asleep was the hardest part: you could hear your guts grinding and then there was this fiery pain in the stomach, ma'am, the cramps made us squirm. But Elías barely swallowed, I'm not going to lie to you, the poor boy was wasting away, really fast, honestly.

Wasting away…

Yes. Very thin. Skin on bones, ma'am. You see, he was traumatised after what happened with the poisoned bird, you know?

Poison?

It was a seabird. We should have realised something was up; it was too calm to be true. One morning we found it perched on the gunwale staring out to the ocean, the same way people stare, with their mind submerged in the water, if you know what I mean?

Yes, Amador. I come from the coast too. Elías was born here, in this little house, the same year they built the sheds for those stinking barrels of diesel on the corner there. I know everything you're saying about the birds. There's no denying when a bird is sick. Didn't my Elías realise?

He helped me catch it. It wasn't hard because, like I say, it was very still. Come to think of it, of all the creatures I fished or hunted, this seabird was the only one that didn't disgust him. We plucked its feathers right

35

there and then. I wrung it out like fresh laundry, you know, to get rid of the excess blood. And then, seeing as the little seabird was only young, just a critter, little more than a chick – you can tell by the soft beak – I gave the whole thing to Elías to help him get his strength back.

And my boy ate it?

Almost all of it, ma'am. I was glad to see him eat something at last. Honestly, after all those days of despair we went through together, I'd started to love him like a son. But that same night, Elías started to vomit, to shake like someone being electrocuted. The convulsions had taken hold of him. That was when I realised it was poison, ma'am.

It seems like you know a thing or two about poisons.

Not a lot. But I did see two guys from the cooperative shaking this one time after being bitten by a 'yellow belly', an enormous sea snake. Anyway, I'd kept hold of the seabird's remains to use as bait, so I poked around in there, between those guts, and my hunch was right, ma'am. The bird was green inside, every last inch. The poor thing had hunted down one of those creatures. Elías was infected.

Go on, Coronado's mother urges him. Amador is surprised that her eyes haven't welled up. She's old-fashioned, no doubt, the type of woman who never cries in public.

I made him drink his own pee for three days, ma'am. There wasn't a drop of rain in all that time, and Elías was dehydrated from throwing up so much. As a matter of fact, after all the medical studies the doctors have done on me, they now tell me that the urine might have protected us from all kinds of bacteria, even the sort that grow in sores on the body.

My Elías had sores?

Just a few, ma'am, mainly blisters on his back, the

kind that burst in the harsh sun, you know? But on the toughest days, we took turns in the icebox. The thing didn't work, nothing on that boat worked anymore, but at least it gave us a way to escape from the sun. As a matter of fact, I even thought of putting Elías in there when he died; it was the perfect size for a coffin.

Tell me, Amador, even though he was just skin and bones, as you say, did you eat my chamaco? Did you eat my kid?

Amador glances at the tortillas and reaches out to take one. He might as well stuff his mouth full of that soft, warm dough and just swallow and keep swallowing, like the drowned man swallows the sea, allowing his stomach to expand, turning its elasticity into a bitter, salty inner shroud. Harbouring the terrifying immensity inside himself as it grows and grows like an absurd erection in the eternal gleam of the water.

Feeling sick, Amador stopped for a minute or two. There wasn't a single sign of human life on this damn boat. The constant hum, he now realised, was coming from the flies. He saw them even before he opened the narrow hatch of the ship's cabin. He scrunched up his eyelids, almost engulfing his corneas, to make sure it wasn't another figment of his imagination. Through the glass, the short flight of those insects was full of beauty. They were flies, most of them blue, and they were emanating from the bodies like some kind of metallic spirit. Amador had nothing to cover his nose with, so he simply held his breath and walked inside. Four men were lying there in the foetal position. Amador tried to move one of the bodies with his foot, but that corpse was headstrong and remained doubled over, like a geriatric or an embryo engrossed by its own formation. The four men were blindfolded, but they were free. They were dead, blind and free. Nothing was tying their limbs. If they wanted to, they could sit up and explain how they had come to be dead. They must have blindfolded themselves, then. Amador crouched down and lifted one of their blindfolds. They were Chinese, Japanese or Korean; he'd never been any good at telling those nationalities apart. But here they were, unaware of their own origins. Were they close to their native land or far away? Had they too been dragged here by a cursed current? Had they, too, dared to fish in unknown ocean regions to catch rare species, white sharks, soft-shell crabs? And what currency would they be paid in, now, for their deaths?

Amador collapsed onto the floor, where, no longer covering his nose, drunk on the smell of decomposing bodies, he too settled into the foetal position, hugging the rope. Perhaps he ought to just give up right there on that levitating boat, give up and die beside those shipwrecked brothers who had set sail from another coast and come to meet him. He closed his eyes. He realised he was crying because his chest heaved like that of a baby at the breast, and he thought about Coronado. Yes, it was better to die beside his admiral. He had to get up, surrender to the water, swim the return stretch and get back to the boat. That was all.

Listen, the woman sighs. The penumbra forms two shallow depressions in her clavicles. Amador hasn't even touched the tortillas yet, because the woman is holding him by the wrist as if to feel his pulse or to hold him back from some imminent danger.

You don't even have to give me an answer. I understand that you could never tell me the real truth. I don't know if you're a man of faith. Do you go to mass? Maybe there, at confession, you can unburden yourself, Mr Amador. Maybe there…

Coronado died on day 95. He keeled over there, along the starboard; the sun was falling onto his back from the left, which meant they were likely drifting south or east. Coronado was coiling over himself, too, like the foreigners Amador had seen on the 'ghost ship'. That's what they called it, a 'ghost', for the remainder of their long conversations. Coronado claimed that the ship had been a desperate invention of his captain's mind; he'd seen him swim, yes, float a few dangerous metres from the boat, but then simply reappear – without turtles, or fish, or anything at all, just paler from the idiotic effort it took to swim under those circumstances.

Is it nice being dead? Amador kept asking him, tirelessly.

And each time Coronado replied that, of all the things that had happened to him in this world, death was the best. It's a light, Coronado would say, without opening his eyes or squinting, because it was surely true; death was surely the kind of light that no longer inflicted wounds, that did not scorch the last remaining cells.

Tell me a story, Amador said, lying next to his admiral's motionless body.

And Coronado, laughing but without moving his mouth, returned to his legends of Japanese swordsmen. Miyamoto was his favourite. The boy had lots of stories about that warrior prince, who could behead a king just as well as chop a fly in half. His sword was like the wind, and while annihilating his enemy, he recited poetry.

That's what the sea had done to them, too. It had annihilated them without for a second relinquishing its formidable purity, those crests of glory that the water raised with a perseverance completely unconcerned with humankind. It was definitely a higher power. Once again, Amador was sure that this was God's embrace and that Coronado had died in his terrible bosom.

One afternoon, not long afterwards, Amador realised that Coronado was missing an eye. The culprits were there, looking smug with their chests puffed out, their webbed feet clinging to the transom where the nets were dangling. No doubt they were still busy chewing that warm, moist eye, soft like an egg. Such

*was the hunger. And what about him? What was he going to
do? How was he going to endure the endless solitude awaiting
him like a kept promise now that Elías was gone? What was
he going to do?*

One of those tortillas, the woman said, is poisoned. I'm
telling you so that you know what to expect. I hope you
won't leave this house without eating one of them, if you
understand me?

Ma'am...

You don't need to explain yourself to me, Amador.
I can imagine what it must be like to experience such
terrible hunger. And to see, there, as if it were a lamb, the
only meat in the world that can save a person. What can
I tell you, maybe I would have done the same thing. It
could have been anyone in your position, I understand
that, and perhaps you didn't choose the fate you were
dealt. We don't get to choose something as important as
fate, Mr Amador. But there were certain things that were
up to you, yes? Those are the things I want to hear.

It was day 102, ma'am. That day, I waited for it to
go dark... To say goodbye... Being left all alone with
nothing but my own voice and my own mind for
company was making me feel sick. I didn't dare to do it
in the light of day. There was no moon that night either.
I stripped him naked. I needed his clothes. The sea was
roaring, as if that monster was hungry too. That was what
was going through my head. We're all hungry, I thought.
And I imagined all of humanity opening its mouth wide
and the void gushing out from its throat like a volcano
of acidic lava. I was going crazy. That's why I kept talking
to Elías, to get all those voices out of my head. He had
decomposed by then, but I got the sense he was still
listening to me. I talked him through my plan. I went

40

into all sorts of detail, telling him how I hunted a little shark and caught it by the fin then watched it die as I stood on the highest part of the boat, watching as it squirmed with despair, like God surely did with us. And while I was cutting up the shark, I offered the softest chunks to Elías; I pictured him swallowing them greedily. I even told him the number of stars I'd just counted. Infinite stars. I never got tired. It was like asking for his forgiveness, it was...

There is no gravestone to put that on, Amador. Where am I supposed to write: 'My beloved son left us, he sank, he vanished on night 102.' Where am I meant to write that? Go on, now, choose your tortilla, please.

Amador slides the plate of two tortillas closer to himself. By now, it's night-time. Coronado's mother hasn't turned on the lights in her house. Perhaps that's for the best. Amador doesn't even need to close his eyes to choose. He's already used to moving his hands, his arms, his breath in the nocturnal waves.

He chooses the tortilla on the left. It's warm enough for him to caress with his tongue, as if to silently give thanks for it. He chews with his eyes closed once again, anticipating his own stillness, lovingly appeasing the pounding of his heart. This is what I am now, the fisherman mumbles, this is what I am now that Elías is gone. And then he takes a bite of that golden tortilla, which the woman has made for him with her own hands. I'm a fish, I'm a turtle, I'm water, I'm the net, I'm a vulture, he sighs, and continues to chew.

IT LOOKS HUMAN WHEN IT RAINS

My heart is a bottomless river,
a raging torrent –
How can I throw my name
into the tempting water?

Yayoi, 16th century

Keiko had been fertilising the soil in the garden all morning. In all the time she'd lived in Santa Cruz, so different to Colonia Okinawa, she'd never had to fill hot water bottles to warm the bed before getting in like she had of late. Now she even ironed her linen smocks over the quilt to take the chill off; as soon as she unplugged the appliance, she would slip beneath the sheets and blankets and use that sensation of comfort, of returning to some perfect place, to think that maybe she should get her act together and go travelling, even though she hadn't saved up enough money.

There wasn't a whole lot she could do about the plants, though. She had tried to protect the garden area from the cold by leaving the porch lamps on all night, but then the electricity bill struck her like a chemical weapon: it exposed a horrific number, a number that resembled an atomic formula, as her late husband used to say whenever he paid the import cheques. She was left with no other option than to soothe her plants with her voice and wish them the strength to survive another frost. She spoke to them like little children, the way mothers talk to new-born babies, turning her voice into the sweetest imposture, an authentic imitation of love. Sometimes she spoke to them in Japanese. She was scared of forgetting that language, the language of the Colony, and so she pronounced the words with care.

For six months she'd been letting out the upstairs bedroom to a university student, but now she was beginning to regret it because that room – converted not long after the death of her husband, since he'd been fiercely opposed to any kind of change – had a glorious skylight which, on sunny days, let in a heat that was constant without being aggressive. When the girl's lease came to an end, she was going to turn that room into a greenhouse. It was a promise.

But it was almost midday and she still hadn't made lunch. The rent included lunch, but the girl could sort dinner out for herself. She was going to keep working for another fifteen minutes while she thought about what to make – the girl always complimented her on her rice, white and loose like droplets of rain. She stopped for a while, hands on hips, to survey her little kingdom of plants, undulating boughs and seeds that lurked in the infantile blindness of the soft soil. No one could understand the pride she felt upon observing the progress of her work. A little bud opening, a minuscule seedling that no one would notice but that was definitely there, with all the vigour of a new life. These were true works of origami, folded so carefully by a perfect, supreme deity, and, try as she might, she could never recreate all those folds and edges. Besides, she had lost dexterity because of that tremor in her left hand, the heart hand, and only if the work was simple – birds in flight, white cranes, red poppies or simple lampshades – did she take on commissions. In fact, the last major commission she'd accepted was for the Japanese association in charge of cultural events at the consular office in Santa Cruz. They commissioned her to make a thousand Sadako Sasaki cranes in foil paper to send out a message of hope, of *gaman* willpower and solidarity to the survivors of the Fukushima nuclear disaster. Two weeks she spent folding the paper, trying to use only the tips of her fingers and not her nails, because part of the elegance of a *tsuki* object lies in the shape of the fold, in the way the line is broken with a naturalness that should imitate the joints of the human body, its linear geometry. She finished the task exhausted and with her fingers in bits, but with a happy heart, lit up by the feeling of *ikigai* plenitude she felt whenever she rustled up perfect flavours in Mr Sugiyama's restaurant. They sent her a thank you letter with a dynastic seal, which she didn't recognise and which troubled her with a pang of sadness.

Back in Colonia Okinawa, when her parents decided they couldn't recover from the floods caused by the overflowing Río Grande, which swamped their vast soya plantations, they briefly considered sending Keiko and her older brother Ichiro to Brazil, where some of the family had emigrated, or to Japan, where she and Ichiro would have to armour-plate their hearts to endure the humiliation of returning. No one who had been so fortunate as to find themselves among the groups of émigrés that embarked on the voyage to Brazil and Peru in 1957 before settling in Bolivia, in the eastern rainforest of Yapacaní, had returned to Japan carrying the wilting flowers of the fiasco on their backs. Fate would have it that their mother caught the plague spread by the rats from the Benian Amazon. Her brain became so inflamed by the encephalitis that her face, of almost childlike features, seemed to be embedded in that vast cranium. No doctor wanted to travel from the capital to the Japanese colony to diagnose the sick woman, and anyone who had initially wanted to help was deterred by the strange rumour that nesting in that woman's head was a giant abscess caused by the radiation that had devastated a region of her home country. The Uruma virus eventually claimed her mother, and little Keiko had to look after Katsuo, aged six months, and help her father with his new agricultural enterprise. This time, they cultivated soya. And in the long run, the soya saved them.

Keiko always liked to think that her mother's *shinrei* had helped them, embodied in the scarecrow they hammered into the middle of the crop field. Each night, after tucking Katsuo in, she opened the casement windows and spoke to it. Little Keiko was sure that the *shinrei* scarecrow was listening to her, because if she asked it for rain, then the next day it would rain. And if little Keiko asked for the rats not to devour the roots of the crops, the fruits somehow survived any such depredations. The era of the scarecrow was perhaps their happiest. And Keiko always had her mother to thank for that. She had promised to stay there, floating like the dew at dawn. That's how she had put it, 'like the dew'. And even when her *ningyô* face turned calm in the bestial oedema of her head, she could tell her daughter that she wasn't afraid, because in that moment, the moment of dying, she hadn't glimpsed any *akuryo* waiting for her to settle accounts. She had been poor all her life, she had crossed oceans with her loyal husband, with Keiko and Ichiro, and she had given birth to Katsuo in the colony. They

46

were the glimmering stars that reigned in her soul. She didn't owe a thing to anyone. Only people with debts to pay must fear that final encounter with Death. Do you understand, Keiko? her mother once said to her. And the little girl understood. So, when a female teacher from the colony gave her that old book of poems by a man named Natsume Seibi – an ancestor of hers perhaps, a wise man no doubt, because only people who had lived deep in the past, between 1749 and 1816, say, could write poems which were like ponds that revealed the reader's reflection – she realised that her mother could be with them in many ways, and not just by inhabiting the body of that scarecrow, made from cotton wool and dry straw. She copied out the most beautiful poem and pinned it over her bed. It said:

The scarecrow
Looks human
When it rains

But now, in the long present tense of her old age, there was no longer room for those flights of fancy, for origami dragons or boats sailing bravely into storms. No more brides or virgins or fierce papier-mâché gladiators. Her eyesight was shot from all that time spent creating worlds out of paper. And yet she had to admit it: in the prison workshop she felt good. Her students weren't exactly artists, but they enjoyed those bouts of creativity while learning the origins of origami, through digressions more reminiscent of legends than historical facts. The women suddenly transformed into children, schoolgirls in their grey uniforms. And Keiko listened to their stories, too. She was surprised to find that she was not appalled by their crimes, their mistakes, their unbridled passions, the gross misjudgements that had led them there. Who was she to ponder their failings. She didn't even dare come up with theories about that thickset prisoner with beetle tattoos emblazoned on both cheeks. Despite the rage with which that woman bore down on the most fleeting moments, there had to be an explanation for her, too; something far more complex than the hasty conclusions other people might draw about who she appeared to be. If her memory served her right, that prisoner was inside for 'second-degree murder' and would have to spend fifteen years behind those bars. When Keiko asked Hiromi, her only daughter, the difference between that charge and 'first-degree murder', the grounds of the lengthy sentence being served by two other inmates, Hiromi had responded sarcastically at first: 'First-degree is to second-degree what origami is to collage: a question of skill.' And then she had explained that the former charge involved neither intention nor premeditation, but rather passion, instinct and the murkiest fate, whereas in the latter, all actions taken were aimed at the total destruction of another human being. Keiko had mentally scrutinised her students' faces, trying to detect a hint of the passion or intent that had compelled them to brandish a weapon, give a push or a shove, strike a match, tear or poison flesh, but all she saw were sorrowful eyes, because despite the sunnier dispositions some of those women had, the truth was that a thin membrane of disappointment tempered the intensity of their expressions.

In the next origami class, Keiko decided to show the inmates how to make a half-coiled snake; she stressed the patience required to score the tiny scales of its skin and, in particular, the extra care they would need to take when straightening the animal's strong neck, conveying the head's bearing of alertness and attack, while the ball of its body remained calm, coiled almost timidly. Three sessions in, it transpired that the woman with the tattoos had created the most beautiful snake of all. Although traditional origami was made from white paper, without glue or embellishments, Keiko let the inmates choose coloured sheets, never embossed or in combination, just pure colours that brought out the character of their creations. The woman had chosen a long purple sheet and had turned it into the most dangerous, most animated reptile in the workshop. Keiko took the colourful snake and gently placed it on the palm of her right hand. She silently paraded the snake around the other students, as if displaying a trophy. And a trophy it was. It was a triumph of perseverance, mental focus and dexterity over mediocrity and the haste of the fleeting, of all that dies before taking a breath. Keiko didn't even praise the sharp tongue sprouting out of the reptile. She didn't make comparisons or ask for comments, like in other situations. To her mind, silence was a simple yet convincing tribute. She returned to the tattooed woman's table and smiled at her. And in that moment, she was reminded of a phrase Mr Sugiyama often used when he wanted to give other people the benefit of the doubt: 'Sometimes life is beetle-black.' At first she was surprised to meet the cold gaze of the inmate she was trying to honour with this ceremonial display; but then she shuddered on sensing that there, in those eyes, where a profound, indecipherable sadness ought to be, was a sinister, accusatory light instead. Keiko let go of that perfect origami figure, as if it were burning her hands.

Keiko continued to hold the workshops, but she was careful to stick to the simple designs instead, the kind that wouldn't require those women to summon a different energy from their spirits. The workshop was supposed to help those troubled minds forget about their confinement for a couple of hours, and she was going to make sure that it stayed that way. She went back to her seabirds, to her swans, jellyfish and owls, which emerged from the paper with three primary folds and a couple more tucks for definition.

Why was it that the plants beneath the vine looked healthier than those others, the ones exposed to better light? Not even the tarpaulin she hung between the posts on the veranda on colder nights had spared these little plants a slow and very sad demise. No doubt about it, Keiko thought, she was nothing more than an old lady languishing over her plants. She ought to feel ashamed, especially since there was so much crime, poverty and suffering in the city; this she had learned from Hiromi, her only daughter. Hiromi hadn't finished her studies, but she had still found a way to pursue her lifelong ambition: journalism. For Hiromi, her father's death had been a liberation. No longer would she have to complete some degree that kept her tied to factory life, the kind of business in which Colonia Okinawa had prospered: textiles, soya, sausages or technology imports. Nor would she have to be silently compared to the other daughter, the one Mr Sugiyama had conceived with that woman who worked for him, the beloved little bastard he recognised as his legitimate child. And nor was she forced to return to the colony, to the north of the province, to do a few days of free labour every month like all the other youngsters of Japanese descent. She could lead a normal life instead. If she had wanted to, she could even have applied for a grant at some Japanese university or other. The Japanese consular office had funded many descendants from the South American colonies, offering them the chance to study higher education courses in that far-off land of plenty. It was an attempt at fixing the broken branches of the great genealogical tree, a way of retrieving those children that had been spat out by the war to parts of the world where they were met by inhospitable jungle, wild water, strange pests, and also, on occasion, love and prosperity. Hiromi, however, felt entirely Bolivian – Eastern Bolivian, camba through and through – and couldn't imagine that any other part of the world could claim her as its own. The young woman had argued that journalism was a cultural calling that had to be nurtured from the outset, and that there was little point in her gaining international qualifications if she wanted to eventually practise in a city where violence was not expressed with the exquisite twists that play out in Japan, but rather in an ordinary way, without poetry – that's what she'd said, 'without poetry' – with no case records of psychopaths that defied all comprehension.

Keiko decided she was going to make Hiromi's favourite dish – pacu with boiled corncob. Perhaps that way she might summon her. If her lodger, Emma, liked it, then good for her; if not, then tough luck, because that was all she was getting. At the end of the day, food and lodgings for 1,600 bolivianos a month were a privilege this little lady wasn't going to find anywhere else. But of course, having the lodger there also meant that Keiko could relax. The girl didn't smoke or play her TV shows and music at an outrageous volume. In the daytime she just stayed in her room, reading and taking notes, and at night she went out to her classes. She was studying literature. Keiko couldn't imagine what that even meant. Reading. As a subject. It had been a long time since Keiko had read anything, even the books from her childhood that she kept in a wooden chest, the ones full of very short poems that could leave a person breathless. She clearly remembered that she had never opened those books feeling that they were something to be studied; it wasn't like they were textbooks. She read them to tremble. With her index finger she would trace the lines of those poems so as not to miss a single letter; that's how brief and dazzling they were, like the little sparklers they manufactured in Colonia Okinawa for a while, until an explosion taught them a hard lesson. Her father had said that that was exactly what it was, a lesson. Gunpowder, in little stars or in bombs, was the worst of the *bakemonos*.

Without the girl around, she had to admit it, that ironic tropical winter would have been less tolerable. It was a shame that her lodger and Hiromi hadn't crossed paths in those nine months, though Keiko had a feeling they wouldn't get along if they did. Emma was of Japanese descent too – perhaps that was why she was attracted to the room – but she'd never lived in the colony, so she knew nothing about the culture. When Keiko showed the girl her origami creations, her eyes opened wide. It was the first time she'd seen a world made out of paper.

It was Hiromi who convinced Keiko to rent out the upstairs room, since she hadn't managed to persuade her to sell the house, that ludicrous house with its conical roof and the little belfry at the top, slap-bang in the middle of that street, in the heart of the town's most hectic neighbourhood, where the street vendors set up shop on market days, dousing the air with the scent of rotten fruit, alcohol and fried food, a tainted breeze that still wasn't enough to put the woman off. When Mr Sugiyama was still alive, they'd opened a shop here selling watches made in Tokyo, where some illustrious ancestors and wealthy relatives of his hailed from. After that, they'd opened a restaurant, then they set up some equipment for developing photographs, ran a restaurant, and then that was that. They were the only stupid Japanese people that existed, Mr Sugiyama used to say, and money fled from them like a rat at the sight of a buffalo. Since Keiko had never once seen a buffalo in all her young life on the banks of the Río Grande, she always suspected that their bitter fate was a manifestation of the ill wishes of Braulia, the woman Mr Sugiyama had been sleeping with while his wife recovered from a difficult labour, and while Hiromi was taking her first steps, with her little shoes on the wrong way round, like a glove puppet, to fix a problem that had been evident from the beginning and would only detract from her beauty. As if the girl didn't have her work cut out for her already, with those little elfin ears she'd inherited from Mr Sugiyama. But of course she couldn't really rely on her own memory anymore because that membrane, the one that held memories and everyday matters, present-day things, was growing increasingly fragile. Sometimes she feared she might break it just by straightening a finger. Perhaps it was better that way, to be left with only the genuine and thoughtful parts, Mr Sugiyama's kindness, the way he'd built this house with terracotta tiles so that she'd feel safe. Her husband had gone to the hammock and mat weavers over in Guarayos and described in vivid detail the kind of rug he carried in his memory as if it were a tangible object. Those people wove the most beautiful tatamis Keiko could possibly imagine. Through all the years of business ventures, the home she shared with that man had been a steadfast light. The idea of turning origami into another source of income only came to her after he died. Mr Sugiyama would have been offended by the mere suggestion. That was why, whenever she spread the sheets of paper across the kitchen table, she always turned his photo the other way and blew out the candles on the shrine. May his soul rise far from all suffering.

The origami classes had given her a routine that sustained her in a different way. She didn't feel any younger, that wasn't it; but the need to use technical phrases to teach a skill she'd been honing since she was a girl forced her out of herself, made her trust in her own words. Hiromi was the one who encouraged her to volunteer as an art and crafts teacher in the workshops at the women's prison, and she'd dealt with all the red tape so that her mother could be appointed and her transport arranged. Keiko went there twice a week, taking her own sheets of paper for them to use. Although her workshop participants were few in number, she prepared as if she were going to speak before a crowd. Some of those women were coarse creatures, more bitter than chicken bile. Were it not for the experience of her workshop, Keiko would never have imagined the sad darkness into which ignorance was capable of subsuming the human will. Those embittered women didn't understand instructions like 'fold down the middle' or 'score a diagonal line'. Around them she'd been forced to re-examine her language, the words she used to label things. Other inmates looked back at her with grateful smiles that did little to detract from the terrible weight of their expressions. The woman with beetles tattooed on her cheeks barely uttered a word. Keiko couldn't say whether her voice was that of a murderer or a cold-blooded killer – she really was intrigued by that particular difference in a person's criminal impulses – whether it was a husky voice or a crystal clear one. Though the latter would have disturbed her, because those sturdy hands portended nothing but thunder. Keiko was still troubled by the perfection of the coral snake created by that inmate. It was a baby dragon on the brink of stirring from its inanimate nature, and it looked as if it had been made with tweezers. But it had been born from those rough, criminal hands. She never mentioned these impressions to Hiromi, because she wanted her daughter to retain the satisfaction of having helped her fill her days sharing the transformative wisdom of origami with others. Hiromi was a good daughter, she was in no doubt about that; perhaps she just needed to gain some distance from this house where, to tell the truth, no one had ever been particularly happy. Tirelessly she reminded herself that Mr Sugiyama had been a good man, a good husband. Whenever something went wrong, the blame always lay with that fourth guest at the table: melancholy, fate, or those symbolic animals Mr Sugiyama always held responsible. The year of the snake, specifically, had been their worst. And that was the part she had tried to bury. Not always with success.

The lodger would be down for lunch any minute. She was hardly likely to complain; the girl barely spoke, but her quiet presence was constant and sort of pleasant, like the light from a lamp.

She propped the bucket and the shears against the last wooden post on the veranda, near the most sorry-looking plants, and she bade them farewell. She'd be back later, she told them, once the sun was barely a ghost, a subtle spectral haze giving way to that other mist, the night air. She dusted off her sandals, scraping her soles against the edge of the hallway so as not to trail dirt inside. Her back was no longer up to the task of mopping the floor three times a week, so she'd started taking much more care with her comings and goings between the garden and the kitchen. Luckily, the soil she used to nourish her little ones was good, loose like her rice, nice and soft, especially in the corner where the plum trees grew. Oh, why hadn't she thought of that before? How stupid! The solution had been there at home all along. What if she moved some of the fertile soil from the plum trees to the dry area, where the sad plants were? She wouldn't have to dig deep, no. All she'd have to do was scrape off the top layer, the part where the dew forms and gives the earth its nourishment, then move it to the dry corner. The earth was tired of draining all its minerals into the same crop; the cycles would have to be broken if the ground was to regain its strength. Then she remembered those basic rules of agriculture her father had taught her while they were harvesting the soya, first by hand, and then later, when Katsuo could contribute his child labour to the colony's chores, with the heavy machinery they bought on credit with help from the international aid projects set up by the Japanese government in the main centres of Japanese migration. It was a simple solution. Use soil to resurrect soil. She would do it after lunch.

Keiko and the lodger ate in silence. Not an uncomfortable silence, but a way for the two of them to pass the time in each other's company. Keiko tried not to compare Emma with Hiromi or, more accurately, Hiromi with Emma, but she had to admit that she felt much more at ease with this stranger, and that if she really thought about it, that was how it had been from the very first moment, when the doorbell woke her up – she had nodded off in front of the television – and she opened the gate without thinking, without feeling afraid despite how dangerous the neighbourhood had become. There the girl stood, with her hair just like Our Lady of Akita, straight, with a centre parting, wearing a light-blue cotton dress that the warm breeze whipped up around her ankles. She said that no, she wasn't the one who'd called earlier that morning after seeing the ad in the newspaper, but insisted she could cover the deposit for the room and the first month's rent. Maybe if Keiko had asked for those documents as Hiromi had advised

– an ID card, photocopies of some sort, employment references and other such credentials that help attest to a person's existence – she would be sitting at her own table now having lunch with a more complicated individual, the kind of lodger who caused the muscles in her back to cramp up, aggravating her sciatic nerve. She was glad to have taken Emma in without much of a guarantee, other than the deposit cheque she hadn't cashed out of a sense of propriety but would of course keep until the contract ended and it was time for the lodger to gather her things (was it really just a backpack…? Oh yes, and a smallish box with a few books in it) and head off in search of her next destination. Before long, the two of them seemed comfortable, bound in a kind of coexistence that was tacit, delicate and perfect like a spider's web, both of them savouring Keiko's fluffy rice. It was over dessert – peaches in syrup and a small chunk of Mennonite cheese – that Keiko asked the lodger to help her dig up the good soil so that she could move it from one corner of the garden to another. The plants would thank her for it. A grateful plant is like a fairy, Keiko said. Emma opened her similarly almond-shaped eyes and smiled. She liked hearing those tales, which she'd never had access to before because she'd been raised by a single mother who was just another cunumi, an uneducated indigenous woman who had only learned a couple of words from the man that planted Emma's seed in her womb. She used to wash dishes in a guesthouse. Emma didn't live with her because the woman had put down roots in her hometown of Urubichá, but also because she had become such a sad woman that it made the poor girl feel useless. Perhaps that was why she had chosen to study literature, fleeing from the dishes, from reality, searching for fairies just as Mr Sugiyama had sought out symbolic animals to blame for his misfortune. And now

Keiko was going to put her to work pawing the dirt. She ought to reward her somehow.

'What do you want in return?' she asked.

Emma got up to collect the plates and take them to the sink. She turned on the tap and lingered for a while, entertained, letting the water sweep the scraps of food away. The girl had a sadness about her too, something that moved Keiko. Perhaps she was worried about her mother. Keiko waited a few seconds for her to answer, then decided to take out a couple of little porcelain cups for some green tea. She liked the hue the liquid acquired in contrast to the gleam of the porcelain.

'What I want', the girl said all of a sudden, 'is for you to make me an origami doll.'

Keiko took a sip of the green tea, trying not to burn her mouth. Her hand was trembling more than usual because she'd been overdoing it in the garden, and perhaps because it was an especially cold day. She had never felt joy or tranquillity folding origami dolls; of all origami creations, those vain little figurines struck her as the least original. Back in the colony, all the girls made paper dolls at Christmas and stuck them onto a polystyrene ring. The white dolls were the new virgin mothers; the brown dolls represented the earthly father, Joseph; and the dolls without any arms, just a head and a worm-like body, were little gods, tiny messiahs whose heads the crafters covered in glitter to denote their status. The girls' parents carried those creations to Santa Cruz, selling them for what counted as a fortune at that time. She remembered those dolls as ordinary beings that held no secrets. She also remembered that it took more creases to make a young doll than an old lady. Quite the paradox, apparently. On just one occasion, too many years ago, she'd made two little twin dolls. She did it to show herself that her *shinrei* was greater than her wounded pride and as honourable and good-natured as her mother's, capable of extending to lowlier things, like the beloved scarecrow on the farm, or to more sublime dimensions, like the dazzling frost at dawn. Yes, she had cut a piece of exquisite paper, like the one used for the pages of the Bible, and with it she'd made two little dolls holding hands, bound together by one continuous fold, like Siamese twins. There was no way she could remember now how she had managed to make a piece like that. She thought this not out of arrogance, but with the astonishment she felt when she pictured her old self, the Keiko who had loved and suffered like any other woman facing the intensity of a man's love. Had Mr Sugiyama loved her deeply? Had he loved her with the fervour of those fires he used to stand and contemplate before checking that the flames of the chicken rotisserie were fully extinguished? Had he loved her like that? Maybe not. From this shameful truth, she had drawn the strength and justification for what happened in the year of the snake.

Keiko decided to use purple paper to give life to the doll Emma had asked her to make. But then it occurred to her that she had left her materials in the cabinet they had allocated to her in the prison's arts and crafts room. The inmate with the beetle tattoos – the wildest one, the woman who insisted on being referred to by her prisoner number even though they were allowed to use their real names in the workshop setting – had helped herself to all the purple paper.

'This one's trying to make a bloodbath!' one of the other women remarked at the time, to provoke a reaction.

Sometimes the inmates roared with laughter, but soon they returned to the calm required for their manual tasks.

The first mound of black earth that they transported in two buckets looked so much like the work of tropical ants that when Emma remarked to that effect, Keiko burst out laughing. Yes, the two of them had almond eyes as black as tar, and perhaps they did resemble a pair of industrious little ants. The things this girl made her imagine!

'Inside,' Emma said, 'beneath the topsoil, they make these really long tunnels. It's the most beautiful work of architecture, so perfect that if you were their size you'd think it was a castle. The tunnels are connected like the veins that lead to and from the heart. The smaller ants get lost in those labyrinths. There are also rooms, little cells, where an ant can stay still for a long time while the others march past in perfect military file. The queen has her own quarters, where she lays her incredible eggs, and the lowlier ones carry food to her. Eventually, when the eggs hatch and the new brood is born, the queen dies. It's always better to be part of the masses, the marching line, because that way you're never alone.

Emma explained all this with such vivid enthusiasm that Keiko felt compelled to look at the ground, at the heap of soil they'd dug up to move from one corner of the garden to another; in that frosty blackness, she glimpsed the invisible life of the ants and felt her chest pressing down on her, though it disturbed her that she couldn't understand why. Whether it was tenderness or admiration, whether she was trembling with old age or emotions, whether it was a bewilderment so different to everything else, that the world would cease to be the same one she had always known. She looked at Emma with fresh eyes, her Asian eyes. Big, ant-like eyes. *China cochina ojos de hormiga…* Wasn't that what the other girls in high school used to sing to her when her father finally decided to send her off to study all alone in the capital? Slant-eyed ant-girl, yes that's what they thought of her. She let them call her 'china', call her 'vietnamita', call her 'japuca', 'nipona cagona', 'ting tong', 'Made in China' and all those other ridiculous rhymes her old memory had been purging over the years. Maybe her lodger had been the target of similar slurs, but then again, Keiko was conscious that these modern times promised a different kind of cruelty; she knew that people weren't so stupid as not to appreciate Emma's stunning eyes, vast like the night. She remembered Hiromi telling her about an outrageous proposal she'd received from a classmate at university once. Ever since she'd heard that tale, the word 'exotic' filled Keiko with rage, with disgust. How truly sad it was to be a trembling old woman. Even sadder to confirm what she had secretly always known: that ultimately she was stronger than Mr Sugiyama. Well, after all, there she still was, asking her lodger to help keep the plants in the garden alive.

Emma wanted to keep digging. In the meantime, she had woven her dark hair into two braids so it wouldn't get in her way. Kneeling there in the dirt, she was no more than a little girl. She picked up a lizard that made no attempt to escape, stroked it for a few seconds, then benevolently let it go. The lizard darted off into the upturned soil. Keiko must have interrupted her right then: she watches as Emma, kneeling on the soil, pardons the little lizard, smiles at her with a vague happiness, and pushes her plaits behind her elfin ears, the same ones Mr Sugiyama had boasted about, saying they were the most honourable legacy of his original family.

It's true, the penny must have dropped for Keiko in these exact seconds, when Emma, her hands full of fresh dirt, looks up and smiles at her. With a clearer head she would have noticed that her lodger didn't feel the cold, even though the southerly wind was picking up and a sprinkling of rain as light and loose as her rice was pattering on their heads, the plants, the eaves of the veranda. But instead, Keiko lingered for a moment on another idea. Like a bird wavering between the branch and the fruit, Keiko delighted in the thought that, when it rained, the world looked good, shrouded by the translucent gauze of the water.

Keiko squints: Emma is now that little girl from all those years ago, the one who knocked at their door, not the house door but the entrance to the restaurant. The woman who has brought her here, Braulia, gives her a gentle push. The little girl says she's looking for Mr Sugiyama. Her cinnamon skin belies her Asian eyes. Keiko feels as if her heart has turned into a machine full of blades, the kind her father bought when they started the noodle factory. Blades that will eventually carve up the organs that betray her pain: the heart, the stomach, the lungs, the ovaries. Everything to do with love, sex, breathing, understanding and forgiving.

The new arrival is carrying a little basket covered with a linen cloth woven in the typical Guarayan colours: a bright violet boldly challenging the golden yellow. Keiko tries to focus on that offering, the coloured cloth concealing the surprise. The girl says it's for her. She holds out the basket with her little arms.

Emma held out her bare arms, still kneeling in the middle of that kingdom of upturned dirt.

'Is this a good amount?' she asked.

Keiko could barely talk with those internal blades hacking away at her. They were one and the same. Emma and that little girl. The little girl. The child who carried the basket so meekly, as if it were an offering. The same little ears. Those eyes.

Keiko takes the basket. The little girl asks for Mr Sugiyama. He's her father, she says. Mr Sugiyama comes out of the kitchen, dries his hands on his apron. He's not surprised. Walking towards the girl, he admonishes her for having turned up in sandals. He'll buy her some new shoes, he says.

Keiko sets the basket down on the table. It probably has bread inside, or squares of that bitter orange brittle the Guarayos bake and sell for a song, unaware of its value, detached from the anxiety inherent to peddling goods for profit. It's so humiliating that this little girl has brought her a gift.

'Do you want me to keep digging?' the lodger asked. Her knees had been sinking into the dirt. Keiko felt her chest loosening with warmth for that girl, who didn't mind getting dirty for her landlady and her dying plants.

The little girl, whom Mr Sugiyama welcomes into their home without consulting his wife, is put up in the same room as Hiromi. 'They're sisters,' Mr Sugiyama declares, 'they're almost the same age and will both inherit the restaurant.' Keiko is starting to get used to that constant back and forth between humiliation and pity. The girl isn't to blame. That woman, Braulia, pushed her into their lives with that basket. There was no bread, brittle or marmalade inside, just a little heap of oblong eggs. The woman who cleans the floors warns her that such an offering could be the work of Guarayo shamans, the worst. She tells her she should bury the eggs. Keiko digs a hollow with her own hands... Where? Over there, where she later plants the cherry trees? In the spot where she tries to propagate a mandrake root that never bears flowers? Where? There, there, right where Emma is kneeling as if she's just awoken from a subterranean dream, that's where she buries the eggs.

'This soil is warm,' said Emma, beckoning her over to the site of her gardening efforts. Keiko wasn't sure if she should move closer to the girl. A strange fear overcame her. The sight of Emma all caked in mud, surrounded by the soft roots that sprouted from the mess of earth, troubled her.

They don't come from a chicken, those eggs. They don't come from birds that pierce the shell with their still-soft beaks, trembling naked, without the slightest hint of the feathers they will later bear. The eggs are scarcely contained by a solid membrane, and she lays them down with immense care in the pit in the garden.

'It's warm, but bitter. You get used to it after a while,' the lodger whispered. Her voice had grown weaker. She seemed to have turned sad all of a sudden. A memory too physical had lodged itself between the two of them. Between Keiko and her lodger.

They are the eggs of a coral snake. Neither the cleaner nor Keiko dares break them to kill the life growing inside. She would have to send them back to the Guarayan woman, Braulia, before evil had the chance to sweep through her home like a shock wave of gunpowder and poison. Mr Sugiyama is responsible for this too, but Mr Sugiyama won't do a thing and will never tell her where that woman, the Guarayan, lives.

'Try some,' said Emma, lifting a small fistful of damp earth to her own mouth. 'It's pure mineral. That's why poor children eat soil. Bodies naturally seek out the things that nourish them. Try some.'

One afternoon, Hiromi and her sister are playing in the garden. Careful you don't trample the cherry seedlings, they're very delicate, Keiko pleads. The girls settle down a little, they lay down on the grass with their arms wide open, like scarecrows exhausted from enduring all the wind and vulture droppings. The girls don't get along badly, but Hiromi still has trouble accepting her sister. Keiko teaches them to make little paper twins out of one long strip of tissue paper. Hiromi always rips the little pair in two. Then Keiko leaves them to play in the garden so there are no thoughts to disturb them. *The family no longer run the restaurant; they import watches from Tokyo these days. The girls will inherit that, a business that marks the passing of the hours, minutes and seconds with hands made of gold, steel and titanium. Until then, in this multiplied childhood, there is no time ruled by ticking hands, so Keiko leaves them to trample the grass nourished with fertiliser, the bones of her plants, the branches held up by faith.*

'Some people use soil to heal their wounds,' the lodger said, her voice increasingly weak but her words still definite. Keiko was saddened by the sight of those knees, still entrenched in the ditch, though the girl herself seemed not to realise the effort her legs were making. Once again, she was just a naughty little girl in her kingdom of dirt.

There is no way to know that Braulia's daughter has been bitten by the hatchlings. The time is 3:59 a.m., according to the pendulum clock Mr Sugiyama has hung on the wall between two decorative folding screens. There are no marks from fangs or bruises on her ungainly body, and her fever is mistaken for the heat of the afternoon, for the games in the garden, for the joy of having shoes to wear, so when her throat closes up and Keiko instinctively pumps her chest, there is nothing to be done. Just then, on the nape of the girl's neck, where the scalp ends and the spine – that perfect filigree work of calcium – begins, Keiko notices two little dots, like beauty spots drawn on with Chinese ink.

'I healed mine,' Emma said.

There was no longer any doubt in Keiko's mind. She knew that this was how it had to be. It was only logical. She looked up and felt the last glints of *komorebi* caress her old face. She wanted to ask Emma whether, in spite of the wounds that the dirt had healed, something was still causing her pain. Not her knees, which by this stage of the gardening chores on such a strange afternoon

65

were surely completely numb; rather, something in her memory. A sense of injustice, perhaps, a prickle of rage at the way her fate had twisted and contorted. Keiko wanted to explain that for this reason, too, origami was a path, a light, because it never resorted to twists or curves to fix a form, but she knew that it was senseless to talk about origami in a transcendental moment like this. And she wanted to hug her lodger and stroke those elfin ears that surely heard so many things in all those years of waiting.

'This has all been one sad disruption. *Shoganai*, Emma, *shoganai*…' Keiko said finally.

Emma didn't correct her. She understood. The time without ticking hands of gold, steel or titanium, the subterranean time of the ant world, had given her another language. Her almond eyes could see what Keiko, too, was beginning to see.

Keiko and little Hiromi are digging a deep pit in the garden. Keiko wails non-stop as she wraps a sheet around the docile, motionless body of Braulia's daughter. And she covers her mouth when Hiromi hurls the first fistful. And she bites her fists and sucks her dirt-caked nails when she arranges flowerpots on that spot until she finds a better solution. That spot. When Mr Sugiyama comes back from Tokyo she'll tell him that the girl has left, that she's taken all her new shoes and just upped and left. She'll tell him this so he won't be so sad picturing the girl in those undignified sandals, the kind that deprive women of their elegance.

'Come here,' Keiko said, struggling to kneel down beside her. She was old for sure, but she could still tell her joints to let her adopt a position, to support her on that final stretch.

Emma rested her head on Keiko's chest. Not even in her wildest senile imagination would Keiko have pictured the girl like this, with the placidity of those who meditate. Emma had grown up and she was there, giving her the aura of her youth. Because that's what it was, an aura, a radiance that had found a way to materialise. It was a *ukiyo* current feeding on the fresh dirt to take the form of a face, two dark braids and a supple body that had overcome its disruption.

Because it had all been just that: a disruption. A nick in the linearity of a perfect piece of origami. A slash in the continuity of time. Wasn't that right? Barely a slit, which they could now mend. And if Hiromi wanted, she could come too; she could kneel down upon that feast of black earth and hug her sister or wipe the moss from her little face.

Mr Sugiyama comes back from Tokyo, and if he suspects anything he chooses not to probe further. Nor does his health oppose the least resistance when an aggressive cancer chews away at his bones, filling them with a cold wind. He consults his books on eastern mythology and accepts that this year will be his last. He closes the restaurant so as not to pass down debts, sells off the few watches he still has, sets up some cheap equipment for developing photographs to leave behind a modest business, and has the leaks in the roof repaired. When Braulia turns up one afternoon to give him a small jar of ointment for the pain, Mr Sugiyama has shrunk several centimetres in height and his upper back is getting ahead of him, giving him a bull-like air. Keiko lowers her gaze.

'The seeds are now the flower... and they only breathe beneath the soil,' whispered Keiko into Emma's right ear. She felt ridiculous for trying her hand at one of those gunpowder poems she'd read a thousand years ago in her books back in the colony. And yet she felt at peace holding the girl in her embrace; she wanted to make up another poem for her, wanted to recite it into her other little elfin ear, pushing back her braid with her trembling hand. A flash-haiku to console her for all this time interrupted, broken, snatched away, to give her something back from the life she hadn't lived. She tried to remember one poem that glimmered in her memory – 'Lighting one candle with another candle...' – but she couldn't finish it, she couldn't find the path that would lead her to the meeting between the seed and its cherry tree. She closed her eyes and took a deep breath of that scent of the girl's mineral hair. She wanted to squeeze her tighter, to feel her vertebrae alive, but she didn't know if she had the strength to do it, or her *shinrei* had already come away. How would she know. There was no longer a way. Only light or darkness, one and the same fold. Darkness and light.

SOCORRO

'Those boys aren't your husband's,' said deranged Aunt Socorro at breakfast, watching the twins as they vied for control of the FlyPro drone, a gift from León that had struck me as excessive.

I smiled, trying to defuse the tension that was pulling my cheeks taut in that unnatural way, much like the Botox I had detected on my mother the moment I saw her. But in my case it wasn't Botox; it was my muscles' tendency to clamp together like useless shields. It was clear that my cheeks, stiff like fists, would be powerless to defend me against Socorro's onslaughts. I hadn't seen my aunt in years, and yet despite my best attempts to identify any sign of deterioration more distinctive than the membrane of time falling across her rather serene features – so at odds with the grating tone of her voice – all that occurred to me was how effectively madness had protected her from the violence of life. How old would she be, that madwoman? Fifty, maybe sixty? I worked out that she must be a decade younger than Mamá, who still refused to disclose the year of her birth, making it hard to establish milestones in that unhinged family of two: she and Socorro, the two of them together since the dawn of time. Behind the steam from her cup of milk – the madwoman drank hot milk with sugar, a lingering remnant of her childhood, most likely – her face appeared to be resurging from a dream.

'Those boys,' she continued, 'are your cousin incarnate. Just look at their chins! And those eyes! Oh, those eyes!'

I didn't know, in that moment, what shook me more: the madwoman's barbed remark or the cackle she unleashed as she spoke those words, which felt like a reprimand.

Why was it so hard for me to sympathise with the poor woman? After all, I had studied clinical psychology in Córdoba before moving to Boston to specialise in 'stimulus thresholds' of boundary perception – a decidedly tedious area both to study and explain – and in my professional experience, which though not exactly extensive was at least consistent, I had succeeded in balancing out my share of extreme psychic structures. Socorro was a straightforward case to classify: the prehistoric electroshock therapy had taken what could have been an isolated flare-up of juvenile psychosis and turned it into a deranged personality, pushed to the brink, essentially. Even so, there was something about the way my aunt used language that unsettled me, forcing me out of a tolerable area of interaction. I felt for the local therapists who'd had the misfortune of treating her, not to mention having to contend with completely ignorant, haughty questions from my mother. Perhaps there was an intentionality to Socorro's perverse statements, something that any of the gurus that had taken to combining certain psychological concepts with that pretentious field of metaphysical thought would call 'malignant' and that I, with my grounding in more conventional clinical theories, was able to identify as 'embittered' or 'negatively euphoric'. Not, of course, the kind of rather nostalgic or melancholically narcissistic bitterness harboured by certain forgotten artists, or by boxers whose brains have been turned to mush but who keep their medals hanging on the walls, dangling from the humble little nail of fetishism. The anguish Socorro exuded was putrid, an incorporeal secretion that transcended her neurological issues (so overrated, by the way). It was with those stratagems of extreme neurosis that Socorro defended the family of two she formed together with her sister, my mother. I have to say, however, that I wore myself out with all this thinking. León had no trouble freeing himself from the obsessions of academic codification, unlike me; even on holiday, I never gave it a rest.

'What are you girls talking about?' intervened León, treating us – well, her more than me – to a beaming smile, so conscious of his manly essence that, for a few moments, it made me quiver like in the first throes of falling in love. Socorro, however, was immune to those sexual impulses, those glints of social libido.

'I was just saying to your wife that those boys are a true copy of the original,' Socorro replied, savouring her riposte. I had to keep telling myself that my aunt had never been in her right mind and, as far as possible, she kept her affective territory to herself. It couldn't be easy to welcome us – a whole clan that, let's be honest, had nothing to do with her – to that draughty house, neglected except for the most urgent repairs. Socorro and Mamá had managed by themselves for more than half a lifetime and were fine with that. Each to her own delirium.

León looked at me, still smiling. He didn't understand a thing, of course, and he wanted me, the expert in lunatics, to translate my aunt's cutting remark for him, to make it easier to understand the atmosphere we were going to be breathing on this enforced holiday. (But who had forced us to come? Mamá had never made it clear that she missed us, yet somehow I saw this summer visit as part of my filial duties.)

There was no time for me to translate. Socorro continued:

'They're the spitting image of the little hanged man, they're his reincarnation,' she declared. And she laughed again, this time with such gusto that Mamá had to come out from the kitchen to contain that whole display of morning insanity; it was only breakfast, after all, and we had a very long day ahead.

'Socorro! Enough!'

At mid-morning we went to the Cotoca Sanctuary, where Mamá wanted to present the twins for Sunday Mass. León and I got into an animated debate on the subject, a disagreement that was saved from becoming a conflict because whenever we went on holiday my husband assumed an all-terrain identity, an ability for self-alienation I envied in him, because in my case, breaks only served to highlight the parts of my life that were populated by ghosts. León would redress the ethical affront to his elaborate atheism back home in Fayetteville, when Mamá's almost manly voice, the voice of a smoker, and the expressionless gaze of the Virgin of Cotoca were no longer around to chip away at his academic temperance.

Socorro remained calm for the first half of Mass and even made the sign of the cross like she was supposed to. She was well trained; she wasn't planning to get on my mother's bad side while surrounded by intruders or enemies. She had already made life hard enough for her sister that morning, when she refused to express her breasts with a battery-powered pump to alleviate the onset of another bout of mastitis. However, after the sermon – a more or less coherent story about Jesus' wrath at the fig tree's inability to bear fruit – Socorro began to grow restless. I recognised the urge to make fists with those hyperactive hands; I considered holding her but feared that the physical contact would overwhelm her. In turns, and without a hint of shame, she began to squeeze each breast as though she wanted to rip it off, trying, perhaps, to return to the most solid and concrete part of herself: her sternum. She also gave off the acrid scent of a rustic cheese that secretes a transparent, slimy whey, like the plasma of a wound. Then, when it was time to shake hands and say, 'peace be with you', Socorro smiled at me so conscious of her own madness that it made me shiver. Or perhaps I was coming down with a cold. A cold, at this point, would be a relief, a cause, a scientific, microscopically verifiable explanation. At any rate, I thought, shifting my focus to her language, to her obsessive rhymes, her serpentine body, a cold was the perfect setting for all the chills, all the trembling, all the convulsions. How psychotic language could be sometimes. I'd had enough. Enough of everything: of myself, of León and his self-control, of Socorro's breasts, of this damn trip. Oh, to be a plaster cast saint, with a solid mass for a brain, hands hovering like doves in a gesture of phony compassion, blue retinas – why always blue? – observing without blinking the pain of others, the gleam of superstition in the desperate eyes of the masses.

Socorro, too, looked at the saints with a curiosity that appeared to be genuine. Was she mentally interrogating them? Was she demanding something from them? For a moment I could see her stripped to the bare essence of her turbulent youth, aged fifteen, twitching at the mercy of those electric shocks, surrendering any real chance at life to those stupid electrode terminals. I glanced at her sickly breasts and those hips ravaged by old oestrogen, and for a moment I glimpsed that psychotic youngster. In our family of women, there was a willingness for convulsion we could barely disguise.

On the way back to Mamá's house, worn out from the trek through the craft market, heads hot from the sun that slicked the dust to our scalps, we decided to stop for a while at a manmade beach on the Kiiye River. The tourism boom had cultivated a whole crop of new restaurants on the wide expanse of beach. There was no limit to the display of paraphernalia for tropical hedonism: jute hammocks strung between the trumpet trees, which could be hired for a couple of hours' siesta; fishing equipment; massages with castor oil; kayak tours for groups or individuals; and even a translator who, for five bolivianos per word, would write postcards in Guaraní and Bésiro to suit the customer's whim. I heard someone ask for the word 'fever' and the translator replied 'akanundú'. Then that same someone paid ten bolivianos more for the sun and the moon. The translator wrote: 'cuarací' and 'yací'. I wondered what the words for entrails, melancholy or panic were. And therapy, too. But I wasn't about to stop and pay for a translation.

If anyone asked me, I'd tell them that 'therapy', in every language, means 'to take out the shit', 'to eat excrement', 'to harvest putrefaction'.

Mamá said the twins deserved a prize for having behaved like two archangels during the folkloric mass. Because it has to be said that if there was anything that made that religious ritual more tolerable, it was the songs and the violin concertos performed by the orchestra, comprised of local children who had studied at the academies in Gran Chiquitania with scholarships for indigenous people. León spent the whole time whispering in my ear that, just as the Holocaust had propelled scientific research, Jesuit evangelisation seemed to have sown the seed for a fresh, untamed and excessively pure talent in those little critters. Hell burns with paradoxes, he said to me at the very moment of the Eucharist, and his voice thrashed my spine like a loving whip. León's intelligence and subtle devilment had always excited me. It was good to desire my husband. The sad thing was not being able to express this desire properly. I kept putting off the need to discuss these inhibitions with one of my colleagues. As long as the emotional dynamics continued at a healthy level of functionality, I thought, there was no reason to channel energy into those areas. Anything else would imply a neurosis far more chaotic than the one that lay dormant, like a structural component of my personality. In the meantime, I carried around a notebook in which I jotted down any uncomfortable stretches. That was what I called them, 'uncomfortable stretches', which I suppose suggested that I was heading somewhere, though I hadn't taken much time to consider where. The thought that just crossed my mind now was the perfect material for those pages of my notebook. It was, undeniably, an uncomfortable stretch I'd had to endure without letting my muscle cramps show. It was what a person – yes, a person, any person – needed to keep propping up the skeleton of a life. Or wasn't that the whole reason why the therapy I had developed, the one I had given a few lectures on in the academic jungle, had been so successful? A delicate alchemy of practicality and the will to keep it all together.

Of course, there would always be some Freudian funda-
mentalist out there to criticise my postulates, deeming
them insufficient and calling their outcomes temporary
and dangerous, incapable of culminating in any form of
liberating catharsis.

But there I was, putting the foundations of my
clinical wisdom to the test, almost resigned to Socorro's
self-dramatisation dictating the next line of the script
to me. I looked at my sons; they would be leaving that
impenetrable puberty behind soon, and I couldn't say
whether they were truly enjoying it.

'It's the perfect day to take your little gizmo out for
a spin,' I said, flashing them the friendliest smile I could
muster. 'There's no wind and nothing but countryside
for miles around.'

The twins took the drone out of its box, and León
programmed it to send signals to the wide-angle goggles
he claimed to have bought for himself, but were really the
final part of his excessive gift to the boys. Being honest, I
had to concede that it was a fantastic invention, one that
had permanently sealed the fate of the prehistoric games
I used to dream of them playing. I wanted to fly it for a
while, too. I hooked up the goggles and tried my hand at
a few simple moves, not daring to attempt 'swoops', 'low
flying', 'zenithal flights', 'abductions', or any of the other
feats of amateur aeronautics that had come to form part
of the boys' increasingly technical vocabulary. From the
considerable heights the contraption reached, I could see
strange angles of the city. I struggled to remember how it
felt to be a natural part of that place. The sense of alien-
ation only became a reality upon returning, not while
on the outside. When the drone opened up that vertical
panorama, it altered the landscape, the planet, life itself.
Of course, it lent it an extra, unsuspected beauty and
made me appreciate my sense of sight in a new way. The

sand of the manmade tourist beach resembled the skin of a giant mammal taking a nap. An elephant or a white buffalo vanquished by the weight of its own mythology. From that vicarious bird, I marvelled at the tops of the trumpet trees, too. They had burst into bloom with an obscenity and a splendour that cast me out. As beautiful as their yellow flowers were – my favourites – those trees were no longer mine. Looking down on them from that magnificent height healed me. That was how traumas and nostalgias rose up, too, with an iron will for detachment. From the sky, the trumpet trees were nothing more than flat platelets that the wind would eventually tear to pieces.

When I completed my aerial tour of those rural parcels of land, I told the twins to take some photos and reminded them to forward them to me by email. I would have time to empty that memory later and not burden my own anymore. I looked around for Mamá and spotted her beneath the red parasols. Socorro was hugging her knees, perhaps protecting her breasts, aching and swollen with prolactin. Her adolescent pose contrasted with her unruly, white, porous hair.

'Let's get something to drink,' Mamá announced, giving two quick little claps, like a flamenco dancer. I saw the delight in her impeccably groomed face when the waiter promptly came over to take our order.

Mamá and Socorro ordered a lemonade each and León asked for a pitcher of draught beer for the two of us. Mamá was going to drive, of course, as the lady and master of the SUV she had started leasing just two months ago, likely confirming her ambivalent status as a well-to-do single woman entrusted with the care of her wayward sister. This scene was not entirely unfamiliar to me. From the video calls on Sundays, and from the times when Mamá had visited us in Fayetteville – without Socorro – I could glean the contours of a life that functioned smoothly in terms of its dynamic, its secret vices, its innermost dirt. From the relief I felt when those conversations and visits ended, I could tell that I lacked the courage or determination to reconnect with my mother and repair whatever it was that we'd once had between us – beyond, of course, the unspoken love that implies duties, like the one in which I was currently engaged.

I took off my shoes. I was calmed by the rough feel of that tropical sand, so different to the silkiness of beaches in the US. The holiday was turning out exactly as I had anticipated. Because if there was one thing I'd gained from my profession – my constant analysis of subjectivities devastated by illusive, slippery ghosts – it was a prophetic ability that, rather than calming me, almost always made me feel bitter. I had been proven right, though: nothing was going to be easy in Mamá's house. I would not experience the thrill of any lost objects from my past – Mamá had given away, burned or thrown out almost everything from my childhood – nor the unexpected consolation of reparations of any sort. They would remain unyielding there, Socorro's rage and Mamá's distant affection, which would not soften, not even around the twins.

I sipped at the liquid slowly, appreciating the healthy, bitter taste of the barley, and I felt buoyed by the certainty that there were only two weeks left; in the blink of an eye we would be saying our goodbyes, dealing with the red tape to export frozen chicken salteñas and the two kilos of charque, the beef jerky Mamá promised us every morning, inevitably conjuring images of smuggled sun-and-salt-cured corpses. Empty rituals which made me immensely tired but which I would perform so as not to trigger any storms.

Mamá and León were drawn into an impassioned discussion on climate change, a conversation that was not without its clashes. Mamá fiercely defended the artificial Kiiye beach. In our time there, León had taken advantage of the opportunity to gather information, ask questions and take photos with the drone, since anything that might lend a touch of exoticism – this was my personal interpretation, of course – to a paper he was working on about a new trend apparently known as 'sensory anthropology' was more than welcome. Mamá was a fount of enthusiasm, particularly in view of her knack for remembering dates. For the umpteenth time, she recounted the climate legend that happened the year I was born, which also coincided with her divorce – 'it drizzled nonstop for two months; the mould spread everywhere, it got under your skin, into your clothes, the sheets, everything… I think we were cursed.' León secretly activated the voice recorder on his iPhone (though his subterfuge was unnecessary because Mamá had always been hopeless with technology). Socorro accompanied the story with special effects, which León recorded as precious evidence of his beloved 'sensory anthropology'. If Mamá said it had rained for weeks, Socorro would click her tongue, mimicking the infuriating sound of the rain Papá had used as an excuse to not sleep in the marital bed. If Mamá said that from inside the wall that separated her old tumbledown house from the neighbour's veranda, they could hear a rasping sound she didn't believe was produced by natural gases in the ancient fabric of the masonry but thought was in fact the call of a hidden treasure trove of pound coins, then Socorro would groan, imitating a murmur from beyond the grave. And when León asked what that word, trove, meant, Mamá and Socorro vied for their turn to speak and to tell the gringo about the ancient tradition through which people bequeathed the wealth they had accumulated over years of deprivation to their children and grandchildren. Sometimes, in dreams, children learned that they would have to knock down a wall to discover, with a relief which pained them, that they had inherited inconceivable wealth. The anecdote reminded me of Freud, and in a way I had to agree with him: we were inexorably tied to the sins and obsessions of our parents, to their buried legacies, to the putrefaction of their inheritance in the bowels of a silent wall swarming with eyes and ears. I needed to get up and take a walk alone along the riverbank.

It was amazing how that feat of tourism had even recreated the thrust of the water, the force of a current that didn't flow into any sea. Or perhaps it did? Perhaps the masterminds behind this universe had also somehow opened up a secret, liberating course to the coast? To think that my twins didn't know what it meant to be raised on a complex, on a fundamental absence. I would always feel bereft of the ocean, and I would always foster the ridiculous hope that the Chileans would eventually ask our forgiveness for that historical outrage and give us back what they had amputated from our country: the water, its true immensity. What madness.

'Why did Socorro say that to you?' León roused me with a start. Half an hour must have passed, and I had been wading deeper into the river, lured not only by the inertia of the water but by the pink river dolphins, which the local council was determined to raise in an alien ecosystem. The smallest ones didn't dare attempt the athletic leaps that the adults performed as though they were being paid an enviable wage, but they were happy to have their beaks stroked, squinting with those beautiful eyes.

'Are you listening to me? Why does your aunt goad you with that subject?'

'You mean the thing she said about the "little hanged

man"?' I sighed. I wanted to stay there stroking the baby dolphins' beaks, but León was pulling me towards the hyper-real riverbank instead. I was trying my best to stay upright in the current. The beer had cushioned my anxiety, and besides, I wasn't going to let León spoil that tiny bit of liberation.

'Yes, the thing about your cousin. I didn't know they called him the "little hanged man" and I'm not sure if I really want to go there. One thing I would like to know, though, is why your aunt called the twins a "true copy". Those were the words she used. Why?'

'Because she's mad, for God's sake, León!'

Mamá, who had always had her uses when it came to dispelling storms, even if it meant piercing her liver with all those lightning rays, called León over to sample the pacu. She had asked for two plates of pacu and one of fried cassava. Mamá never tired of pointing out that pacu, that indisputable privilege of the Amazon, an amphibian god found nowhere else in the world, was fantastic for the libido. What must she have seen when she looked at us? We weren't a pair of nymphomaniacs, for sure, but the frequency of our encounters was about average – and I of all people should know that, having treated so many intimate pathologies in my time. I had to admit, of course, that it had been five years since I had scheduled a session of emotional 'reorganisation', but that was because the colleagues in my immediate circle had made an embarrassing pact with pure psychiatry and its psychotropic dealings. Solitude, I was coming to realise, was inveigling its way into many levels of my life.

'And call the twins over too, tell them to put down that demonic device for a while,' Mamá commanded. Around us, she didn't have to hide how much she loathed technology. She managed with the apps on her smartphone, but that was as far as it went. She had even paid a tourist agency's fees to get to Fayetteville and had traversed the airports in a wheelchair with enormous sunglasses shielding her eyes so that no one – given the ironic statistics of airport encounters – would recognise her.

'Demonic!' Socorro bellowed, plunging into another obscene burst of laughter, one of those low-decibel cackles that set my hair on end. Her breasts wobbled, dousing her shirt. I was disgusted. But that wasn't going to be enough. Ranting and raving, she strode over to the spot where the twins were commanding the remote control of their post-human machine, then she muttered something to them that I didn't quite catch. I saw her take Junior by the chin and hold his face gently, as if to get a better look at him. I couldn't say whether what I felt in that moment was a defence mechanism or some kind of ridiculous jealousy, jealousy for a madwoman choosing, in the Russian roulette of her battered psyche, a potential object for her affections – an impossible process of projection and introjection. And yes, by virtue of the binary system my two sons comprised, the object she chose would have to be my polar opposite. Of the two of them, it wasn't Junior that had inherited my wide-tipped nose and the distribution of my features. Junior looked nothing like me; a different gene pool surfaced in him. But Junior was the one Socorro had held by the chin, singing to him in a voice so off-key it seemed to wallow in its chaos: *amorcito, corazón, yo tengo tentación de un beso… compañeros en el bien y el maaal…* Then, once again, the burst of laughter that destroyed the world. Any possible world.

It was too much. I did the math in my head and concluded that we had enough money to pay the airline's fee to bring the flight forward. I decided I wouldn't mind arriving into some huge airport and driving across all the

82

bridges in Little Rock. Surely there'd be space for us on another plane. I could already see the four of us cruising across those skies of return and liberation.

The mental decision had given me some relief. When we got back to Socorro and Mamá's house, I felt my muscles unclench a little. I leaned against the window and closed my eyes. The last rays of sun were sure to open my pores, which I had taken the opportunity to 'seal' with three sessions of laser treatment in the cosmetic paradise of Santa Cruz. But I didn't care. Let that dirty sun get in; maybe it would shed light on something I couldn't see. Something, a body or a sofa over which my memory had laid a white sheet. I made an effort, I waded into myself the way I had waded into the river Kiiye; I cobbled together the lost pieces of old puzzles. I groped around in that darkness for the silhouette of the 'little hanged man', as my aunt had so shamelessly called him, turning that diminutive form into a horrible transgression. I could only remember his eyes, Lucas's eyes. Not his face, not the shape of his mouth, all his different expressions, just isolated features, the way one might recall a trauma. I saw the mathematical birthmark between his upper lip and his nose, at such an equal distance it seemed that faces carried their own fate. Lucas's eyes. The left iris forever open as a result of that brutal, senseless motorbike accident – perhaps his first suicide attempt – and the right, which, trying to balance the light that invaded his brain through the wide-open door of his damaged iris, contracted. Many times I tried to convince myself that ultimately he hung himself not because of me, not because of what they said about his origins, or his history, or the unwanted heritage that would eventually reveal itself in his blood, but because of the excessive light that was surely cornering the neurons in the vault of his poor cranium. Yes, that was it: the guilty party was the light that violently burst through and scorched that fantastic grey matter, the brain with which he had loved me and written songs for me. The secret forest of his brain must have been riddled with shadows.

We decided not to have dinner, we were so exhausted. Socorro was complaining of pain. Mamá stripped the robe off her like someone preparing for an exorcism.

'You'll pump your breasts or I'll lock you inside!'

Socorro scrunched up her face, but immediately abandoned that retractable expression and launched into her little performance of crying and self-pity. Mamá snatched off her sister's bra with a move worthy of a karate fighter. Socorro's sickly breasts were so swollen that they didn't even slump in defeat.

'Why does everything have to be so difficult with you?' Mamá spat at her, dialling down her tone, almost sweetly. Socorro wandered off half-naked. The woman was a barbarian.

I got the twins off my back with a bottle of Coca-Cola and some bread rolls with butter.

'For heaven's sake,' Mamá scolded. 'That's bricklayers' food.'

That night I awoke with a fever. I groped around the floor with my toes, but all I could feel were the cool tiles – where had I put my slippers? León was sleeping with heart-warming abandon. I fumbled blindly for León's slippers, too, but then I remembered he had an indestructible fungal infection. I decided to make my way into the kitchen barefoot. I crossed the yard with quick steps and I realised what all adults discover: that the yards of childhood shrink with the years. The little mandrake – which, Mamá explained, had finally blossomed after all the years of obsessive care Socorro had given it, fertilising its roots with banana peel – produced a horrible, pungent odour that was scarcely attenuated by the moisture of the lemon tree, which barely bore fruit anymore. I turned on the lamplight in the kitchen so as not to cause a racket at that time of night – what time would it have been? Five o'clock? Dawn's darkest hour? – and I looked at my surroundings to survey this sudden familiar map. I knew that Mamá kept medicines in the drawer next to the cutlery. She had always hoarded them. So much so, that the first thing León did when he arrived was throw out all the expired bottles and blisters he found. Mamá had watched him as he did it, her heart gnawed away at by the feeling that she was being pillaged. It would have hurt her I'm sure, each of the pills that León tossed into the bin with playful marksmanship. Didn't each tablet, each tiny capsule, light blue, golden or purple, antibacterial, antitussive or calming, hold the perfect promise of another world? Of course, that was what my professional rivals promised. The same easy, artificial escape I had always argued against. Still, even I was willing to pay a fee to change tickets to flee Socorro's persecution, her incomprehensible cruelty. Planes or capsules, milligrams or miles – they were all a means of absconding.

León had been so thorough that all I could find were fruit salts, little half-used tins of minted ointment and vials of diarrhoea medicine. Not a single aspirin.

'What's the matter?'

I gave a start and instinctively clung to the cutlery. The long bread knives and the thick knives for chopping chicken were in their wooden block next to the blender, out of my reach.

Socorro's face covered in Nivea creme – I recognised it by the unmistakable scent – really brought out that deranged expression. (Perhaps it was that cheap, heavily fragranced cream, rather than the sublime peaks of madness, that had kept her suspended in the purest time, free from the anxiety of a cyclical existence.)

'I have a fever,' I told her. I needed to give her a swift response, something to establish at least a semblance of logical conversation. The anxiety that talking to my aunt caused me was boundless.

'Let's see...' said Socorro, waddling towards me. An addle-brained zombie in more sense than one. She reached out and, in a maternal gesture I never suspected from her, held the back of her hand against my forehead.

'Ay!' she exclaimed, 'You're burning up!'

I smiled. Her reaction had been genuine. I can't say it was affection, exactly, that her over-the-top display made me feel; no, it was the small pleasure of the performance. One of the exercises I had always enjoyed using with long-standing patients was dramatisation. I would ask them to roleplay individuals that posed a problem in their lives, and in almost every case the mask slipped, the shadow retreated, the pain throbbed like a skinned animal. That wasn't what was happening to us in that faraway kitchen, but Socorro's urge to occupy a maternal place in relation to me had produced an unexpected reaction in me. Tenderness? Nostalgia? There was nothing there, no debris, no emanation or shadow to merit such feelings. Nothing of me remained in that house.

'There has to be something in here to stop the burning,' whispered Socorro, and the word 'burning' took on its true meaning. It was the same word she had used during her most critical phases, a few years back, when she had insisted on denigrating Mamá to anyone who would lend an ear. She claimed that Mamá had forced her to have her womb and ovaries removed, that her sister had 'hollowed her out' to stop her ever falling pregnant with a 'pup' again. Strictly speaking it was true: Mamá had authorised a total hysterectomy to save her sister from cancer. In stark terms, Mamá was the only master of that embattled body in which my aunt sustained her pains. Socorro, however, believed – also justifiably – that there was a different motivation for that internal amputation. My father, her sister's husband, had 'had his way' with her. That was what the madwoman repeated from her post at the front door: 'He had his way with me,' she said. And the neighbours gawked at her with a mix of condescension and morbid curiosity. Socorro had never got a single fact wrong. She was the statistical archive for everything that ever happened; she remembered the dates of birthdays, ages, and the exact time of events – weather or family. So if Socorro said that her brother-in-law had 'had his way with' her, then there was probably a thorn of truth poking out from behind her unhinged tongue. We never spoke about this, of course. I found out from my parents' rip-roaring rows, confessions so clamorous they lost all their vital mystery.

Socorro opened the top drawers and the light from the kitchen lamp made her nightgown transparent. Once again I could see her large, sickly breasts, breasts that had had to forego natural milk – so I thought – and that were now becoming swollen with the terrible, collateral milk produced by certain psychotropics. The left one was especially full, but Socorro had won the battle of the afternoon and had flatly refused to pump it, despite the threats from Mamá, who told her sister she was going to have her milked by a bulldog puppy.

When Socorro emptied the plastic container of blisters and sachets, I noticed a gentle industriousness in her movements. She wasn't always clumsy; if something genuinely moved her, she could overcome the sad, numbing effect of the suppressants. I studied her face more closely. The Nivea cream had been absorbed and, beneath her shiny skin, I could detect the same bone structure that Mamá, she and I shared. The rounded chin that mellowed our faces and lent a touch of softness to our eyes and our fleshy, worn eyelids; the tip of our noses, which was anything but a tip: it was an indomitable will with an unfortunate tendency to implode. I felt an irritating knot in my throat.

'They wouldn't let *me* see him,' she said, just like that, while her hands organised the pills from the plastic container by colour (that was the method Mamá had come up with to prevent her sister getting intoxicated if, for some reason, she had to administer the medicines herself).

I remained silent. I knew who she was talking about. I wanted the madwoman to shut up right there and then. I wanted the holidays to be over and for them to let me go, with my husband and my twins and their demonic or divine machines that were looking prematurely at the world from above, with precocious arrogance.

'I can't tell you that I was certain,' said Socorro, releasing a cat-like hiss as she sighed. Was it possible that my aunt still got nervous, even under the influence of all those chemicals? I remembered a historical essay I'd once read about some herbs used to treat the mentally ill in olden times, herbs so powerful they loosened the muscles, even the vocal chords, producing a gruff, animalistic voice. Of all the voices and almighty laughs I had heard from my aunt during that visit, which was really hers?

'When do you mean, you weren't certain?'

'You know, that night. When I walked into the bachelor pad. I was taking his dinner to him because he wasn't allowed to eat with us. You know your Mamá hated him. It was such a bother for her, having to look after an orphan nephew, even though she'd watched him grow up ever since that moment. That moment!'

'What moment, Socorro? From the *very first moment*, is that what you're trying to say?'

'I'm not trying to say anything. Never say anything, wasn't that right? Yes, that's right. Don't say, don't cry, don't laugh...' Socorro picked up a dirty glass with dregs of Coca-Cola in it and performed on the innermost stage of her memory. 'Clink, clink, went the lemonade. I think I'd made it without sugar. I wanted to punish him too, so I took the lemonade to him without sugar, poor little pup of mine!' Socorro laughed and her breasts jiggled. I feared she was going to unleash another of her seismic peals of laughter, but beneath everything, under all the layers of her voices, the cell walls burst by the drugs and the dregs of that sickly milk, that beautiful ray of intuition was still there.

'Why did you want to punish him?'

'You were gone by then, you'd left three months earlier, and everything was fine in our home.' That was what Socorro said, 'our home', banishing me from that place even in her historical account. 'Lucas was always nice and quiet so as not to bother your mamá. But then you called. Do you remember calling? Do you remember?'

'I remember,' I said, opening up the possibility of some kind of memory or delusion, I couldn't be sure which. So intense, all the images that Socorro hurled at me like vomit, like an arc of vomit from a liver in metastasis, the kind of bile that can cause hallucinations and requires the very same medication used for borderline patients. How fragile the balance of it all.

'You said you were pregnant... You told us there were two of them. Two. And I thought, two's better than one because there's always a chance something will go wrong,' Socorro burst into laughter and then squashed her breasts together.

'Nothing was going to go wrong,' I replied, as if protecting the past from the prospect of any ill omen.

'Then it was me who had to tell him. Someone had to tell Lucas. I thought it would make him happy. What a beautiful thing happiness is when you're young. It burns all over,' Socorro laughed again. 'How was I to know that the pup was a bit stupid? Stupid, stupid!' Socorro was still laughing, but now the tears were gliding over the Nivea cream and soaking her nightgown. 'I should have known; I saw the two of you the night you married the gringo. There, in the little utility room,' Socorro pointed to the room at the other end of the yard for dramatic effect, behind what was once the waterwheel pond of clear, deep water and had been turned into a circular island of potted ferns dominated by the foul-smelling mandrake which had recently come into bloom. A yellowish bulb kept that utility room in the place where I wanted it to stay.

'You saw us…' I said, slowly. My throat had sealed up and I needed a glass of water. It was a cold coming on, definitely. I took the glass from her hands and I drank a sip of that watered-down Coca-Cola. I looked around for a chair. Socorro remained standing with her legs slightly apart, perhaps the way weary soldiers do.

'I saw his spine with all the little bones, folding over you like a prince. You were for him and he for you. Who said that people aren't made for each other? "They're brother and sister, despicable woman! Don't you realise that, fool?" she spat in my face as if to wake me up. But she was the mad one!' Socorro burst into a huge fit of laughter, a roar of pure vertigo.

I wanted to beg my aunt to stop telling that story. I looked around for an object, a fetish, something that might serve as one of those *objets trouvés* in films, the kind that awaken from their insignificance and change the course of things. The knives were still in their wooden block. The discoloured bulb plunged the utility room into exactly what it was: a tomb. The twins' drone was lying defenceless on the kitchen counter. Perhaps if I invited Socorro to fly the machine, to look down on the city from an unreachable vantage point, all this terrible remembering would evaporate once more into its necessary haze.

'And then I walked in with the lemonade without any sugar, nice and sour so his blood would get some vitamins, lemons are full of vitamins... I walked in and he wasn't there, in that room he called his "studio". Someone had broken his electric guitar in half. Broken! And it wasn't a thief, because the cassettes with his songs had been disembowelled, too, and the photos were all chewed up, and the letters, your letters, shredded like with a grater. I went out to the yard, I looked in the waterwheel pond because that pond was dangerous – Chocolate drowned in there, remember, the dog you brought home from the park, we couldn't tell the colour of its fur at first because he and the mange were one and the same animal. You were a very good girl, you... I loved you... But this time the pond wasn't to blame. Quiet as a mouse, I made my way into the utility room. Pitch black. That's what it's like in my dreams sometimes. The dark studio, the dark laundry room. But I had to turn the light on. Do you walk into rooms without switching on the light?'

'Socorro...'

'I switched on the light in the little room and the first thing I saw were his feet. They were like Jesus Christ's. You saw Jesus in the Cotoca Sanctuary, didn't you? That's what his feet were like: scrawny, pale. That's why I prefer to look straight into people's eyes. Feet make me sad. The next thing I saw was his face... That purple blotch, all the way round his neck. But even then, he still wasn't ugly.

And it's a lie that they stick their tongues out. My little hanged man's tongue wasn't swollen. And he was looking at me. At least I think he was looking at me. Oh, those eyes! If not me, then who would he be looking at? You're a doctor, you should know who they're looking at.'

I wanted to get up and give Socorro a hug. She was Lucas's mother, after all. I wanted to stand up, I really did. Only once had I touched a patient in therapy, and I wasn't sure if it would be a good idea. But Socorro wasn't my patient. She was my aunt. She was Lucas's mother. I kept telling myself this, ordering my knees to help me sit up, to help me support my spine, my muscles, steady my restlessness. Stop and walk. That's what I kept telling myself, unable to understand why I was still sitting on the chair, my hands clasping its edges.

It was Socorro who reached out with her saggy arms and took hold of my head, the same way she had done when she stroked Junior's chin and face. My stiff neck resisted. Socorro pressed down harder on my temples, as if she were trying to feel my thoughts. In an instinctive act of self-defence I took hold of her wrists, as if I too were trying to gauge the blood pressure of her thoughts. But she and her madness were stronger than me. She lifted my head to her chest. The madwoman was sobbing. Or was it me? My neck was still trying to resist that sudden dominance, she playing the preacher casting out demons and I acting the possessed woman defending her evil nature. But a part of me wanted to give in. I tilted my head to the left, trying not to bury my whole face in that bovine chest. It was impossible to hear her heart beneath it all, beneath the purulent flesh of her breasts. What I could feel, though, was her soaked-through nightdress – from milk or tears – gluing us together as she overpowered what remained of my defences.

'Neither you nor I were to blame for anything,' the madwoman said. 'I hope you don't forget that.'

My hands were still holding onto her wrists, but by then I knew it was to control my shaking. I was afraid of tumbling straight into her abyss. But I also wanted to drown there.

'Neither you nor I,' she whispered sweetly. 'And Lucas even less.'

I let my whole face sink into her nightgown. I stuck out my tongue, I licked the fabric, maybe sucked it, so that Socorro's stale milk might soothe me a little. Or so that it would infect me once and for all, dragging me forever out of reach of sanity with its turbulence.

DONKEY SKIN

It goes like this
The fourth, the fifth
The minor fall, the major lift
The baffled king composing Hallelujah.

Leonard Cohen

My name is Nadine Ayotchow and I've been singing in the Niagara Church gospel choir in this beautiful town of Clarence for many years. Thirty, or something like that. I don't have a favourite song because they all help us to express different moments of this existence so full of trials and falls. But if you insist, I really like *Hallelujah* by Leonard Cohen. My life has been exactly what he pronounces in his prayer: 'the minor fall'. *Hallelujah* is a song that takes me back to the incredible years I'm going to tell you all about in our assembly today.

I have a little house down by the river, but I come into town for choir practice and celebrations. I haven't always lived in Buffalo. Before I made it here, to the home that the Lord had planned for me all along, I had to live in cold houses, in trailer parks, in poorhouses, shelters, basements and the backs of trucks. I should also tell you all that in the prehistory of my life I lived in the heart of South America and I was meant to be someone else, but the Lord's work on my existence brought me here and everything has worked out well. God took my heathen fate and turned it into this procession of calm days. It's true that the fear is still there, but it's also true that I have my voice to sing and fend off the fear. There's no other way to get it out of my head. I know that in a few days, when they extract that pernicious growth, the one that rises from my pituitary gland and lies in wait for my pineal gland, the Lord will defend my talent, my song, and maybe the most important pieces of my memory, too.

I'm grateful to our preacher, Jeremy, for joining me for this talk. I feel so overcome... No, that's not what I want to convey... It's such a great honour to know that you consider my treatment a case of medical importance. I wish I'd prepared myself better to tell you this humble story, but Preacher Jeremy insists that time, too, is a gift from God, especially in my case. You all know me, and you know that I'm not a well-read person, my education is only modest and it's based, above all, on the spiritual values that the Niagara Church has taught me over the years. That's right, I really enjoy the short books from our *Theological Canon*. Their language is simple, and the examples of major triumphs over the weaknesses of this existence are astonishing. Those little books keep me company and inspire me with wonderful ideas that influence the subjects of my dreams. There are phases when I dream of my mother often; then for months I forget about her and devote my time to dreaming of animals, of new lyrics for hymns, or of long and winding roads. I dream a lot. The doctors haven't figured out whether this abundance of fantasies is related to my glandular disorder. I must confess, though, that this symptom doesn't worry me.

We should always be grateful for abundance, even if the true nature of it escapes us. Dreams, fantasies and memories are all part of this unique wealth I possess, and though I inevitably confuse them sometimes, that doesn't mean I think of myself as a foolish person. The truth is, these flashes of the soul aren't all that different to one another. Close your eyes for a few minutes and think about what I'm saying. You'll find you agree with me.

The doctors on the medical team investigating my case insist that sharing my biographical memories with the brothers and sisters of the church – the memories that prevail in my consciousness like fulminant smudges of a beautiful but unfinished painting – will stop them sinking into the contaminated fluid of my brain. That's exactly how I picture that threat: a jumble of confused cells poised to drag the individual episodes of my story along in their wake. Preacher Jeremy has explained that to testify means to let go of the most authentic parts of oneself, and that letting go is a fundamental step. This is a step I want to take before they operate on me. And what better than to do it for science. I never was any good at science. Well, you already know that I never finished school and that everything I know I learned from that great sacred book. All the wisdom I need is in there. For a while, sure, I tried to find that light in cocaine, and I'll confess that, yes, there were moments when I felt really good. My sorrows drifted away with the smoke from the crackpipe. I'm so sorry to have to tell you about that experience, but if there was one thing I wasn't willing to compromise on, it was leaving that part of my journey out. What a sad thing omission is.

Long before I found my little house here in Clarence Hollow, I spent some years in Canada, in a region encircled by frozen prairies, a place with a similar landscape to our village but a very different spirit. Although Preacher Jeremy doesn't really agree with what I'm saying, I'll say it again anyway: towns, mountains and cities all have their own spirit. The chain of events continued in that place, in Manitoba – the accidents that the Lord used to bring me here, to this atrium where I talk to you each Sunday and lovingly perform songs of glory and praise. Songs that have healed me.

We must be wary of chance occurrences, coated in innocence. They're the delicate pieces of a puzzle whose whole only reveals itself after too many years have passed. If a piece is missing, you might find yourself at the bottom of a river or under the spotlights of a stage, which is exactly how I felt the first time I sang professionally with the gospel choir: I felt as though a benevolent hand had grabbed me by the scruff of my neck, like a puppy, and rescued me from the depths of a swamp. You see, rivers can be wonderful and ominous, and that's why I still need them. Forgive me if I jump around as if between the stones on a path as I bear witness. I've never been much good at keeping things in the right order; sometimes I reveal the outcomes first or I confuse them with the causes. It's a symptom of my illness. The two were always connected, but there was no way I could know it. Right now, as I share my testimony with you, I think that perhaps the Nadine Ayotchow speaking to you today is the wrong part of me, the fate that wasn't meant to be. Forgive me, dear doctors, forgive me, Preacher Jeremy. You wanted me to focus on my spiritual healing, not on my doubts. So that's what I'll do:

We were just kids when Aunt Anita took us to Canada. Our parents had died in that horrible accident on Death Road, in the Bolivian Yungas, and the house where we'd been happiest was still mortgaged. There was no inheritance, and no safeguards or timely prophecies. The only blood uncle we had left in Santa Cruz, Papá's brother, said that children were always better off being raised near a female voice, and so without saying a word, he signed all the migration papers needed for Dani and me to leave Bolivia and his life for good. Being Bolivian is a mental illness, he told us in that good-humoured way of his, which made us forgive him for everything, even for handing us over like pets to Aunt Anita, who, when the time came to appear at the juvenile court, despite all those breath mints she slotted between her teeth, still couldn't disguise the stench of whiskey.

We arrived in Canada in January, can you imagine. The worst month to start a childhood from scratch on the prairies, beneath the soft sobs of the snowflakes. It was like dying.

Aunt Anita rented a house that was falling to bits. Its high ceilings provided shelter for pests, and there were patches of mould on the exposed beams. It's a historical gem, she repeated constantly, looking up at the rotten rafters. That first winter we had to sleep on either side of her huge body to endure the cold that seeped through the walls and windows. In spring everything will be better, and then in autumn, paradise! she promised. But spring came along and the ridiculous garden that surrounded the house was an embarrassment. The snow had only just begun to thaw, and though Dani and I shifted the dirtiest mounds, not a day went by without a fresh layer of gritty mud threatening the vegetable patch Aunt Anita had started to cultivate. The clapped-out pick-up truck we drove to the stores in Winnipeg to stock up on groceries skidded whenever it set off, each of its outbursts kicking up a fresh batch of mud outside the house. To console myself, I imagined the quagmire was melted chocolate and Aunt Anita was the white witch of the forest. That was Mamá's favourite fairy tale, because of its romantic French beauty, she said, and its forests and desperate little children. I often pictured Mamá that way, lost in the rainforests of the Yungas, dragging her long hair through the springy grass, marking the trees to help Dani and me find our way when we went looking for her. It was a shame that Aunt Anita had had our parents' bodies cremated, even though she insisted it meant they could travel with us wherever we went and we wouldn't be burdened with the pain of other immigrants, who are left to imagine the deterioration of the graves where their relatives are sleeping. They carry whole cemeteries in their hearts, she said, whereas we can take Sophie and Carlos in our suitcases and cauterise the roots of our homeland once and for all. There's no such thing as homeland, she used to say, it's a construct, of course it's a construct! Our family comes from a race of exiles and we love our ancient misery, she used to tell us. Dani and I didn't understand a word.

Aunt Anita and Mamá never came to feel like Bolivia was their home. When all was said and done, Papá was the reason they were there; he had taken Mamá with him after they got married. He met her in Toulouse, and, although she didn't shave her armpits, he used to say, she was incredibly beautiful. Aunt Anita was beautiful, too, but the chronic sadness that had plagued her since she was very young had formed deep folds in her milky face and glazed her eyes with the sheen of a sick animal. It was enough to look at the photographs in the album Mamá had treasured and compare them with the eternal present tense of Aunt Anita's sagging face to realise that the woman's ravaged appearance was not the work of genetics but of the unfathomable volume of misery she carried around. Whenever Aunt Anita stared at me after dinner, I knew she was analysing me, checking to see if that malignant spirit was nesting inside me, too. She wasn't all that concerned about Dani, because she used to say that if the malignant spirit was nesting inside him, the worst that could happen was that he'd turn into a drunk, like her! The main difference being, a drunk man would always have a woman to rely on, someone to take off his boots before rolling him into bed. I don't think Aunt Anita ever realised that Dani was queer. Forgive me, Preacher Jeremy. Or perhaps she did, but chose not to talk about it because she already had enough on her plate raising us. Her only other experience of bringing up little ones was limited to cats, she told the staff at Immigration when we reached Canada, but those *orphelins* (meaning Dani and I) need me, they're my *neveux*, mine, I can't just leave them out in the cold.

The first afternoons, when we had just moved into that fossil of a house, I cried a lot. I knew that Aunt Anita had never been in her right mind because the whiskey had been corroding the cells we all have in our brains, the ones we need for our basic bodily functions: walking, breathing, talking, sleeping, going to the bathroom, even laughing. Back then I didn't know that just a drop of whiskey was enough to destroy your tongue, the roof of your mouth, and your throat. Judging by the way Aunt Anita closed her eyes as she took little sips of that liquid, anyone would bet she enjoyed that fiery sensation.

Did I mention already that there were mornings when I used to wake up asking for my mother? I'd call out for her just as I opened my eyes, when the sound of the faucet dripping or the oil making the egg white dance transported me back to Santa Cruz. It was hard to tell those times apart. No one could know that even then, my confusion was due to the diseased growth that was slowly climbing along the base of my brain, intent on infecting my pituitary gland before covering the tiny pineal butterfly that connects the two hemispheres. Aunt Anita would snap her fingers at me to summon me back to this new life, without Mamá or with only her ghost. I don't think I brought this up before, did I? And it's important that I do, because if not then I forget or it pops up like some bizarre spring when it's no longer relevant, and in a testimony there has to be some kind of logic so that the person listening can take something away from that other lived experience. The disease took hold of my brain, but gospel music has granted me the grace of healing. And I owe this testimony to you, to my brothers and sisters of the gospel. There is no gospel music without community. And just like the choir's song, where the vibration of a single voice should be almost indistinguishable from the force of the whole group, my personal illness, too, can help science find a cure.

The first hymn I sang was *Crossing the River Jordan*. That was when I discovered that when it comes to telling the same story, the accumulation of sound and beauty is more important than individual harmony. Be it in falsetto or insisting on improvised soul, gospel music invites you to let go of your ego, to allow your own voice to flow into the others. Like making a home-made saline solution: water, and salt in the water, assimilated but recognisable all the same.

Where was I?

Oh, that's it. Mamá had forced her sister, Aunt Anita, to leave Paris and move to Bolivia with her because she was tormented by the idea of leaving her sister alone in a loft overrun by cockroaches, without anyone around to supervise her treatment for alcohol addiction. *Elle est mon sang!* Mamá had argued in all her fights with Papá, who could smell the dangers of sharing his home with a dipsomaniac. That was the term he used for her – dipsomaniac – which only served to confuse me, because I couldn't help but associate the sound of that word with truly disgusting or incomprehensible images such as cannibalism, vampirism, the resurrection of the dead, and other things that I didn't dare confess to Mamá.

Aunt Anita never did adjust to life in Santa Cruz, with us, because Papá couldn't stand her. Every day my father confirmed his devastating assessments of her moral integrity, saying that nonsense was one thing but pretension was another. No one with half a brain was going to believe that Aunt Anita had taken an aristocrat as her lover. This 'Lord Auch' she harped on about was a product of the unstoppable delirium tremens she had made of her adulthood. Our poor father never imagined that that woman and her dipsomania would end up in charge of Dani and me.

With delirium or without delirium, Aunt Anita still became our guardian, although her hand had trembled like crazy when she'd signed the papers in the juvenile court. And now, in Canada, with her voice trembling too, she kept telling us she was doing her best to 'save our hides'. It was her favourite phrase. Especially when we didn't do things her way. She used to say it in French and in Spanish, and in both languages it made me shudder.

On the darkest nights, when I could make out the shadows of the mountains or the reflection of the snow on the walls of the house, the fear invaded me the same way that the cold sweeps into the nostrils, the ears, the throat and the soles of the feet. Even today, I still can't be sure if the bolt of white electricity that shot up my neck and settled into the very centre of my head was another symptom of the pineal disorder; what I felt was a kind of light-headedness, the sense that a shove was all it would take to hurl me into an abyss plagued by darkness. And the certainty that the darkness would eventually suffocate me.

I wet myself at the mere thought of Aunt Anita taking herself at her own word one day – 'God knows I'm doing everything I can to save your hides. *Dieu sait que!*' I pictured her possessed by the turns of phrase that came out of her mouth; and grabbing the knife she used to scale fish from Lake Alice, she would peel off our skin without shedding a tear, and then, marvelling at her feat, she'd hang out our freshly washed skins to dry on the wire fence. No one would take the story to the police, for the simple geographical reason that our dilapidated house stood on a small plot of land adjacent to the Métis settlements, and the people there preferred to solve their problems a different way.

At first sight, a Métis could be dark and shy like the Ayoreos of Bolivia, or pale and direct, with translucent eyes like any other gringo, but once you got to know them you understood that though they might be a little crazy, they went to great lengths to avoid problems. When Aunt Anita told us we'd be moving to a 'historic' house in an area that neighboured the Métis settlement, Dani and I prepared ourselves to put to use the sign language that Mamá used to communicate in the deaf-mute school and the few kung fu chokeholds that Papá had taught us in case we needed to defend ourselves in exceptional circumstances. Our ignorance ran as deep as those clean, open mouths that the ice formed on frozen lakes. Those gaping holes are a real danger, they can gobble you up in a matter of seconds without so much as a bubble. We imagined that the Métis would have no spoken language, nothing that might serve as a bridge between us. But soon enough, we realised we wouldn't be needing any of that – no sign language or self-defence moves; those people were more civilised than Aunt Anita herself, who was always drunk, belching and farting like someone from a circus sideshow. And it wasn't true, either, that the Métis were in a centuries-long war against the white folks. Street brawls, pushing and shoving, that's all it was, the kinds of scenes we'd occasionally witness in a market or near the barbed wire fence, when some white guy turned up in his truck to spit on their ground or claim cattle from them; but even then, there was no need for the authorities to intervene.

The blame for these outrageous and completely misguided expectations Dani and I had of the Native Americans, whom Aunt Anita sometimes called *les tricheurs*, lay with the people we'd met during our first two months in Vancouver, when we stayed in the home of a woman who smelled like rotting meat. Laughing, that old woman told us that the Métis were still savages; it made no difference if their children went to state schools now or if they occasionally mixed with the whites and even thought of themselves as a nation. They were dead set on regaining their atavistic roots, she said, getting back to who they were before the French turned up with their filthy sexual fantasies and sowed their seed in the wrong place. What else was to be expected from that depraved mix? The old ones were the worst, that foul-smelling woman said, not just because there was no way of working out their age (given that they reincarnated even in this life) but because they hadn't changed their ancient practices one little bit. Even the children could scalp you and leave your brains throbbing in the open air, without harming a single nerve cell!

Aunt Anita spoke French to some of those people with Oriental eyes – who were anything but Oriental – and that was a surprise to us. I had never imagined that an indigenous person could speak French. I had never been to Canada before, I knew little or nothing of its secrets or powers, and it was clear that many things happened differently there. Sometimes I wondered if, in fact, our aunt had taken us to somewhere far more remote. A corner of the earth so unknown, it was almost another world. A place that seemed normal but that made you look at yourself with different eyes in the mirror of the frozen rivers. I'm saying this because all it took was for some old guy, the kind who sat for hours fishing touladi on the banks of Lake Alice, to open his mouth and fill your head with legends of spirits of animals and Independence fighters that hadn't been honoured with a fitting tribute. In many of these legends, the Métis heroes would take a knife or use their own hands to skin their enemy or pluck out his still-warm heart. They weren't the least bit ashamed to repeat and talk about such exploits on a radio programme that aired on Sundays, when they answered telephone calls in French and English. And in Michif too, of course. Aunt Anita listened closely to those stories based on real cases of violence, revenge, spite, and allegations of intimidation and hounding with hocus pocus, and she changed everything to suit her own taste. A taste that had a weakness for whiskey, unprovoked bursts of laughter and the commonplace horror of newspapers; when she was in a good mood, she called herself an 'horrorary member of the Agatha Club', a Sunday column detailing the biographies of serial killers. Sometimes I think she would have really appreciated the little books in our *Theological Canon*, they would have given her the intensity she needed. Shame no one ever offered us that nourishment back then. And if I asked her for a bedtime story, she would eagerly turn to her twisted tales, explaining to me, her voice hoarse from the 'twilight tipple' she drank to loosen her varicose veins, that she'd never told a single lie in her life; thanks to the alcohol, she'd been able to live her life as a completely honest person, far removed from all hypocrisy – this she insisted, her voice shaky but proud – and she wasn't about to start lying now, when she'd been tasked with raising two minors that *la vie dure*, without asking, had placed along her arduous road. So I had to make do and enjoy the journalistic and radiophonic horror she recycled for me, because this also strengthened my willpower and my spirit, and eventually helped me to conquer, once and for all, my inexplicable tendency to panic. Not even she, a woman capable of drinking herself completely senseless, had experienced that horror vacui – *D'horror vacui*! she used to cry, full of impotence, staring at my gnawed nails.

Aunt Anita did lie, though. She too had a weakness for beautiful lies. Beneath her headboard she kept a book of poems by Georges Bataille. 'My Shadow Bible' she called it, that book, which she took hold of as if it were some demonic object that had to be grabbed by the horns. Early one morning, when Dani and I got up to look for a bucket to deal with the hammer blows of a leak that had wrought havoc on our room, we saw her through the crack in her door, frantically rubbing herself down there with one hand while holding onto her dark bible with the other. And reading, too! She was reading to herself, but pretending that her voice was someone else's, a voice that spoke to her with mercy, authority and seduction, like Jesus Christ to Lazarus – forgive me, Preacher Jeremy. I'm sure you will all understand that I cannot repeat those lust-filled verses my aunt read out loud, at least not without drowning in the brazenness of it all. The most decorous line she recited is one I still hold in my memory: 'My mouth implores O Christ / The charity of your thorn.' And then she slumped back with a sigh. The poems from the shadows were gone and she lay there completely still on the rusty bed. It was only then that she noticed our shadows on the lino and called out to us. This is *la petite mort, ma chérie*, she said.

These days I think that she was right all along, as dramatic as it may sound, because she had already detected this void in me, a void that not even the Lord can mend – forgive me, Preacher Jeremy. I'm talking about the millimetric distance between the sella turcica and the minuscule tumour that the doctors have found in my brain. According to the diagnosis, this tumour is trying to find a niche, and were it not for the gospel music and those high-frequency vibrations, it could have devoured my pituitary gland and pared down my pineal gland until the two hemispheres collided and everything went dark. Of all the possible niches, trust me to have the kind you find in graveyards. Sorry, brothers and sisters, that was meant to be a joke.

Yes, it's important to have a good sense of humour. In our gospel sessions we learn that songs are sustained by high spirits. Songs of praise, real ones, should make the happiness of the soul resonate. Technique helps, too. Breathing. Inhale and expand the diaphragm. Let the notes ring out, supplying the air calmly. Did I already mention that these breathing techniques helped to ward off a seizure? There you have it: the scientific miracle of the Lord. I don't think I've stopped to talk about that yet, the core of my testimony. The way that gospel music kept me alive, despite my illness.

It was Dani who had to explain to me that Aunt Anita's efforts to 'save our hides' had nothing to do with us being skinned alive. She was trying her best not to be a coward, and she was prepared to raise us on the outskirts of Winnipeg, one way or another. That day I was ashamed to have doubted my aunt's kindness of heart. I too had given into those two words Mamá used in defence of her sister: suspicion and prejudice.

Those first few months, despite the brutal winter and how badly I missed Mamá, were a beautiful time. Aunt Anita made dinner at seven every day, almost always pasta, and Dani would light a fire and we'd snuggle up together like cats. Aunt Anita asked me to sing for her; she said the best thing about me, the thing that might save me from prostitution or perhaps lead me to it, was my voice. You could be the soloist in a cathedral choir, she used to tell me. Maybe she was a prophet and the world, in its foolishness, had merely failed to pick up on her clairvoyance. That's how proclamations come about sometimes, shrouded in alcoholic fumes from a dirty mouth. I would sing until she joined in with her shameless voice and ruined the whole thing. Then we'd collapse, defeated by the weight of the day, which was an incalculable weight, a blind stone that settled at the nape of the neck.

It was a series of minor incidents – the start of the spring with its disarray of dirty snow, the rheumatism drugs, which Aunt Anita swore were *placebo pur, mon Dieu!* and the visit from that red-headed woman who spoke in fragments of French and Spanish – that put her in a terrible mood.

Anne Escori? the woman shouted. The glass with its dry dirt tattoos made it almost impossible to see the visitor through the window. Her voice, mind you, was full of authority, like a history teacher selecting her prey in class. Anne Escori was Aunt Anita's name, her real one. In fact, it was only people in Bolivia who knew her as 'Anita'; even Papá used to refer to her as 'Anna', stressing the double 'n' to make it clear he was addressing her as a foreigner. Aunt Anita never corrected him, but she did point out that she preferred the cutesy name that the maid and the neighbours liked to use to refer to Sophie's French sister. They didn't even realise that the woman's brain was completely muddled by the alcohol, it seemed.

Anne Escori? Are you in there, Anne Escori?, the woman shrilled.

Is there anyone living in this house? the woman insisted. Dani had climbed onto the toilet to watch her from the small window high in the wall. That bathroom may have resembled a prison, but when you waited for the warm water to puddle at your feet, you wanted to stay there a while after a shower to keep your blood pumping.

Is she with the police? I asked, just a hunch. None of us had committed a crime. Well, not yet. Or maybe Aunt Anita had a really ugly past in Paris. I remember Mamá and Papá talking about our aunt's long spells in hospital after an awful case of alcohol poisoning; they praised the healthcare system in France, not to mention the new developments in rehabilitation; they were incredible, zero electric shocks or religion, they raved, no incarceration, at least there was that. Perhaps everything she'd been subjected to in the clinics in Paris had driven her to crime. On one occasion she'd threatened a pharmacist, demanding he give her some really dangerous pills without the necessary prescription. She was carrying a paper knife, and although she explained that she intended to use it on her varicose veins, to stop the muscles in her poor legs strangling her, she ended up behind bars for a couple of days, crying out for a little sip of something, anything, even just some disinfectant. That was the day

Mamá decided to take her to Bolivia for good. I suppose it must have hurt her to be parted from her lover, this Lord Auch, if such a love affair existed beyond the confines of her troubled imagination.

But we were in Canada now and the woman was still there, yelling on the doorstep of the house.

It's got to be about the mines! Dani said. Perhaps they've heard about that tiny diamond we found! I hope you've hidden it under lock and key, Nadine. Make sure Aunt Anita pulls a brush through that matted hair. Go, run!

The redhead knew nothing of the tiny diamond Dani and I had found among some rocks, inside the Métis settlement. All the woman wanted was for the two of us to go to school. She spoke Spanish to make sure Dani and I understood too, though in truth we spoke and understood more French than we let on; it was a way of keeping our armour on, an instinctive decision that we'd never discussed. That woman gave Aunt Anita a month to come up with a solution, since it was obvious that neither the lake that separated us from the Métis settlement, nor the little snow-topped mountain range that whipped the back of our house with its icy breeze, nor the bare birch trees that spoke to me in sinister whispers, were going to teach us algebra or history, the two main subjects that any university required, that woman said, not only in respectable Canada, but in the US or Europe too. Besides, the woman insisted, it was important for us to learn English or French properly, ideally both languages, and not to just settle for a dribble of words that would make us seem like newcomers all our lives. Spanish was always welcome, but wasn't it a good idea to integrate? Even those people you share a border with, Madame

Anne Escori – the Métis, the Inuits or any other citizen of the *Première Nation* – send their children to the cities to get a decent education. It's my duty to encourage you to reflect on this. *Les enfants* pick up French fast. French, wasn't that the language spoken by the maternal side of their family? That's the only way they'll really be able to feel at home here.

At home? Aunt Anita asked. Her chin was shaking like it did when she drank too much.

Or for as long as they live on Canadian soil, the woman replied, a little exasperated.

Oh, wow. It seems there's no place in this world they'll leave you in peace, huh?

What do you mean? the woman asked. And I noticed how she clung to the yellow folder she was clutching against her olive corduroy skirt, nicely ironed, smooth like those pool tables that the Métis rented out in their farms in broad daylight.

Nothing really, Aunt Anita smiled, dewy-eyed. I thought that this would finally be enough to move the woman, but in all likelihood our visitor, being an adult, could tell the difference between the emotion of tears and the aqueous membrane of alcohol.

Okay then, the woman huffed and puffed, coming to her feet and taking a good look at Dani and me, I'll be back in a couple of weeks to see how things are going.

The woman put her hand under my chin and looked into my eyes while squinting with her own, perhaps totting up the similarities to determine how exactly this ethylic woman entrusted with our guardianship was related to us.

This girl has one pupil bigger than the other, did you notice? the woman said, making a circle with her thumb and index finger in case Aunt Anita failed to understand what she herself had noticed with a single glance.

Her eyesight is fine, Aunt Anita said, not particularly sure of what she was saying.

It might be something, though, the woman told her. I'd advise you to have a doctor take a look at it. And I'd advise you to get a telephone line installed somewhere in this house, too. It's a peaceful area, but a home should have some means of communication, you know, in case anything happens.

What could happen? Aunt Anita asked, observing the harsh light that made those sky-blue pupils intensely transparent. It was as if one could see the future in those delirious corneas.

The woman didn't respond, perhaps because she understood that our aunt's question wasn't meant for her and she wasn't going to find what she was looking for in those incredibly pale eyes – no answers or solutions, not a semblance of responsibility. Just memories of Paris.

From that day on, Aunt Anita's body grew heavier. The way she dragged her slippers along the lino floor was a sight to be seen; it was like watching a dejected astronaut. She barely read her Shadow Bible and no longer listened to the radio. The malignant spirit had such a vulgar hold over her that she'd stopped showering and washing with rose milk to get rid of the crust of dirt forming in the folds of her fat neck. She began to resemble her foul-smelling friend from Vancouver, the one who had welcomed us into her home when we first arrived. But that woman had an excuse; she was suffering from rosacea. A map of raw skin spread across her back, and even the sticky aloe vera gel she used to soothe it did nothing to improve that aroma so similar to meat that's gone bad.

My hallucinations of Mamá took a turn for the worse. It wasn't like I could see her at the table having breakfast in the morning or silhouetted against the fire from the hearth – they weren't those kinds of visions. It was the sheer force of memory, of a time that didn't move forwards like it does naturally, but that kept returning, again and again, to an earlier point and settling in like a small, solid certainty, the size of a pea, like the pituitary gland that defines our whole sense of harmony and our emotional well-being. If the three of us hadn't been so affected by the loss of Mamá, then Dani or Aunt Anita would have realised that this obsessive repetition of memories on my part wasn't a quirk of our childhood bereavement, nor a temporary side-effect of the sudden orphanhood, but rather a clear sign that lurking there, where Buddhism believes we cultivate the sacred lotus flower, which is the will for spiritual transcendence, was an invisible, silent disease.

Whenever this happened, a sadness blacker than the sky getting ready for a storm hovered over my head. I tried my best not to cry because that was like giving wings to the malignant spirit. Aunt Anita used to say that the malignant spirit was thirsty and drank tears. She would have made a great catechist here, in the Niagara Church, because she could make you believe the most extraordinary stories. In those days, before getting into my sleeping bag, I used to slyly take a little sip of her wine from the biggest demijohn, not just to heat up something inside of me, but as a way to sterilise whatever was making its nest there, in the same place where my colossal fears were growing.

On afternoons when Aunt Anita was sleeping as if she were dead, Dani would take me to a thin slip of river that peeled off the formidable Red River, whose banks were strictly out of bounds to us. The narrow river, on the other hand, was inoffensive; not even its most turbulent eruptions burst its rocky banks. Sitting on the stones, we would watch the first shoals of fish that rose from the warm currents. We didn't want to stay home because the dry birch trees that were silhouetted against the crumbling living room wall morphed into macabre skeletons that danced towards me and filled me with terror. There was no use in Dani getting me to look at those trees over and over, to convince me that the bare bones I saw were just the branches flayed by the cold. I had always been scared of everything, and this life with Aunt Anita had only made my fears worse. Looking at the water, I could cast off my thoughts and let them slip away with the current or ford the stones. To me it seemed inconceivable that Dani couldn't see what I was seeing. After all, we were brother and sister, weren't we?

Odd patches of ice still floated on the river, and Dani lured them over with a stick. Sometimes they broke and sank in seconds, like sharp daggers. Other times he managed to drag them across to us and used them to look at himself, like in a mirror. His reflection levitated in the water. His hair had grown; he pushed it behind his ears and smiled. I swore to him that he was just like Mamá. And I wasn't lying. Dani was beautiful like a real girl. Please forgive me this admission of vanity, Preacher Jeremy, dear doctors, brothers and sisters of the Niagara community... Back then I looked at him and thought that we had been born with our identities switched. Wasn't it suspicious that our names were just inverted syllables? In those days, my brother was called Daniel and I was Nadine. I know he used a different name later, just as I adopted a stage name when I started recording gospel music. Aunt Anita used to say to Mamá that toying with our fates like that was completely fiendish. Dani and Nadine, Nadine and Dani. She was right. Instead of taking after Mamá, with that dainty little nose and those eyes like a Japanese doll, I resembled Papá in almost every respect, especially my large mouth. Back in Bolivia, everyone said it. Even Dani made fun of my big boca, calling me 'bocota' or 'bocaza' when I really made him angry. To add insult to injury, I'd started to gain weight uncontrollably – not that matters of the body really concerned me back then – whereas Dani had shot up and was developing muscles that gave him the air of a Greek god.

It was one of our last afternoons there, on our way back from the river, when Dani told me that it was time to leave. I felt my heart skip three times, like a frog. Three years had gone by, and I'd started to think of the winters, the thaw, our trips to the stores in Winnipeg, and our occasional visits to Saskatchewan in summer or on warm days, as a welcome routine that balanced out my fears. The waking nightmares, the wizened claws of the birch trees scraping the wall of my room were never going to disappear; instead, they attached themselves to the rest of my life, or what had become of it then. Although the home-schooling system had solved the issue of our formal education, Aunt Anita's disastrous health was an entirely different matter. But she, too, was part of that cold, sometimes lukewarm life. The thought of leaving hadn't even flitted into my fantasy-filled head.

We're going to leave here, Dani pressed on, gnawing at one of the first blades of grass of that spring. You still have that diamond, right?

But Dani, I said, always such a scaredy-cat compared to my big brother, diamond smugglers go to prison. Didn't you hear them talking about it on the radio? That boy on the news was the same age as you, and they're sending him to prison for selling illegal diamonds… Aunt Anita says the blacks' market is dangerous, it's…

The black market, stupid, Dani butted in. Anyway, that's not where I'm going to take it. They only sell Native American babies there. We can sell it in the US as soon as we get there. Can you imagine, Nadi? We'll enter through Rock Island, through the Great Lakes. Or maybe we'll go to Saskatchewan and work something out. Petite Mort says another option is to head down to Ontario and get in through Niagara Falls. We'll have to really think it through, Nadine.

Leaving… I sighed.

We can work in a restaurant somewhere and save money, then take it from there. If we stay here with Aunt Anita we'll never have a dime to our name. When we finish school she'll have us working in some store in Winnipeg, you can be sure of that. What does she give us in return for everything we do, huh?

Bed and board, I said, like a parrot mindlessly repeating her words, because that was the phrase she brandished like a rusty old knife every time Dani loafed around in bed until after nine.

We'll have that and more, all by ourselves, Dani said. He was hot stepping it between the withered trees as if someone were waiting for us somewhere.

But don't you feel bad for auntie?

Bad? Have you seen how she sleeps, belly up, without a care in the world? She looks like a bear! Dani bent over slightly, puffed out his flat belly and slowly made his way through the fresh spring grass, making sounds I was sure no bear ever made.

I laughed and tried to convince myself that deep down it didn't bother me that Aunt Anita might be left to spend a thousand winters alone in that fossil of a house. She'd be fine as long as she had the placebos for her rheumatism and the smuggled bottles that some Métis gave her in exchange for products she brought home from the towns. All I asked was that the truck would keep working forever. Let her have that truck left in her life, at the very least.

Dani, still playing the bear, walked towards me and then stopped, just like the young she-bear we'd encountered many months before.

If you stay here, Nadine, you'll turn into a drunk old pig, just like Aunt Anita. I'm getting out of here, with or without you. I'm going to leave. Petite Mort will cover me with the truck tarp, I'll travel in the back with the horses. We'll never be rich in Canada, Nadine. Think about it. And think quick, because I don't have much time. They're getting a consignment of horses ready. I'm going to go with them.

What about Bolivia? I asked. For a few seconds I imagined that Mamá would be there waiting for us. Her long hair and her French songs that spoke of unreachable moons.

Bolivia? Dani smiled, with a sharp, ironic look I'd never seen in him before. Bolivia is a mental illness. Did you forget that, Nadine?

That night, sitting on the swing suspended by chains that had likely been used to enslave people centuries ago and that screeched like something from a horror film, I started to do what Dani had asked me to: think. Make a decision. I listened to Aunt Anita rattling the dishes in the kitchen and I caught sight of her in snatches, like in a dream, because the steamed-up glass and her constant pacing made her seem farther away. She moved slowly. Her legs criss-crossed with varicose veins made me feel pity. She was a weary old she-bear with an eternal thirst for alcohol. I realised that my imagination had been shifting, because in the inner world of my dreams, the landscapes had changed too. I no longer saw Mamá dragging her long hair through the grass of the Yunglas. The trees of Santa Cruz, most of them short, had given way to impassable mountains, lying on the horizon. The creatures I'd once found familiar and amusing – the parakeets and the hyacinth macaws – had disappeared, too, and a new fauna had come to populate my desires. Bears, foxes, crows, deer and coyotes, their shadows or their eyes with that direct, sometimes sweet expression, featured daily in my fantasies. Did I really want to leave, now that there was some kind of order that allowed me to live with my everyday panic and all those silhouettes that the slightest change of light traced on the surface of things? The new reality that surrounded our fossil of a house had come looking for me and had done me no harm.

Sitting on that little swing, I remembered the time Dani and I saw a she-bear, a real one. It was an afternoon, in our second year in Canada. Dani and I had been to the Farmers' Market, out on the part of the prairie where Manitoba ended and the countryside opened up to vast, rolling hills, just before the start of the roads towards the capital. When we came back with bottles of wine for cooking – the only thing we could buy with my brother's ID at the time – Dani told me I had to see Luna Sangrienta and Petite Mort taming horses inside the wire fencing of the settlement, that I'd love it. Those weren't their real names, of course, but when Dani spoke to me, that was how he referred to the only friends we'd managed to make in Manitoba. They were actually called Kenya and Mistah, like anyone else in the new country. Our new friends' names weren't twisted like ours. Where had Dani plucked those nicknames from? It was clear that the sight of Aunt Anita spread-eagled, having touched herself like that while reciting lewd poems from her treasured book, had made a mark on my brother. This is *la petite mort*, she'd said, her features contorted with pleasure. And Dani, taking a liking to that phrase, had used it to baptise his special friendship with Mistah. And Luna Sangrienta? I could have sworn my brother had plucked that name from my nightmares. Preacher Jeremy told us how Joseph saw abundance and famine in the Pharoah's dreams of cows, do you remember that? Fourteen cows in total, if we do the math. It was possible that Dani had used the indigenous tricks he learned from his friend Mistah to enter my dreams and keep me company, to shoo away the chiaroscuro images my pineal gland was painting. In one of these dreams Mamá appeared before me, dusting her dress to remove the fresh dirt from her grave and shaking the seam of ashes, her own ashes, from her jet-black hair. Mamá returned holding a large book with a hard, shiny cover, and just like that – with her hair all dishevelled in her eagerness to come back to life – she told me a story. She opened one of the comics Papá used to collect. Come here, Nadine, she said, sit on my lap and I'll tell you the story of a group of soldiers from the Pampas of Argentina. Although this soldier's name was Juan Martínez, she said, his enemies called him Huinca Negro, and his daughter, the little girl born with an exquisite port wine stain on her right eyelid, they called her Luna Sangrienta, 'Bleeding Moon'. The little Luna Sangrienta, Mamá told me, was not ashamed of that birthmark, because in her family and her tribe everyone painted their faces to mark the occasion, whether for a holiday or to go fight on the plains.

Of course there was no way I could prove that Dani had stolen that name from me. Invading others' dreams is a shameful act. In dreams, the intruder can see all our true desires and everything that fills us with horror like an unstoppable flood. Poor Dani could probably no longer remember our parents' faces, which would explain his need to ransack my secrets. Dani wanted to see our parents too, he needed to tell them what was happening to us in Manitoba, where Aunt Anita was beginning to wash her hands of us and drinking herself senseless instead, hugging her demijohn as if it were a man.

The day we saw the she-bear, I reminded Dani we weren't allowed anywhere near the most private part of the settlement, where the Métis had set up a casino that people said awful things about. Aunt Anita cut her own little deals with the Métis, but the difference between that and the two of us going up to their cabins and farms was astronomic. That afternoon, we stayed on the narrowest edge of the riverbank, where we could barely make out the trailers, the bars and thrift stores and the barns where Mistah protected the thoroughbred horses from the freezing blizzards.

Do all those horses belong to the Métis? I asked Dani.

Almost all. Some of them are only here for a while. Petite Mort is training them.

Training them? For what?

To compete in races or to behave better for their owners.

Dani went into great detail about Mistah and how he trained those horses, the way he spoke to them in his language and the horses understood him, how he groomed them while serenading them with Métis songs – which, according to Dani, were the most beautiful the human ear had ever heard – and then gave them water to drink from pitchers where the ice floes were melting. He said he rode those horses in the early hours before the harshest thaw, which happens when the sun comes up. Dani told me Mistah was his friend, that he had this incredible mane of jet-black hair and he was very manly because he could bathe in the freezing water of the lake with barely a shiver, letting the water buff his chest, bristle his black nipples, glaze the tattoos on his pelvis, and so on and so on... Dani wasn't ashamed to go into detail; he even told me all about Mistah's penis, how it was wide and had the head of a hungry cobra... Forgive me, Preacher Jeremy. I just want to make it clear that my brother Dani couldn't help but feel that attraction, it wasn't up to him. It's all in the pineal gland, I'm sure of that. And the pineal gland is the camera of human happiness, capturing every single impulse in its purest, most honest form, like a flight recorder on a plane. The Lord, our ultimate Creator, was merciful to give us a diamond like that in the middle of our heads – even if it arrives damaged, like mine, that doesn't matter.

As I was saying, this was the conversation Dani and I were having when suddenly we saw the bear. She was grey, with a white back and chest. We could tell right away that she was only young – pure instinct, not a vicious animal – and yet a single swipe of her claws would be enough to slit both our throats. But she stayed still and stared at us the way humans do, trying to get through the other person's skin to find out what's going on inside their neurons. Like an encephalogram, which I've had done many times.

I could hear my brother panting. He always did that when he was happy, and also when he was nervous. Dani would have made a good gospel singer, too.

Nadine.... my brother whispered. I squinted, and he said the same thing he always used to say when I didn't like scenes from actual reality: that it was a dream, and that if I reached out to touch the thing appearing before me, my hand would pass through the air, my fingers would occupy the void, and my body would move forward in the empty space. That's what I was focused on when the she-bear's terrible groan pierced my chest like a blast of icy wind.

Sa maeñ! someone growled. It wasn't the she-bear, of course.

Dani was barely breathing. His friend Mistah had stopped the she-bear with a single command. My hand was still outstretched just centimetres from the animal, but she looked over at Mistah as if recognising an owner or a big brother, the same way I looked at Dani whenever he got me out of a sticky situation, no doubt; then she turned around and disappeared into the trees, with a swiftness I would never have imagined from such a large mass of fur.

Mistah lowered his shoulders, as if deflating. He told us it was lucky that the 'natural beast' hadn't gone for me – this was what I understood of the mix of Michif and French he used with my brother – because if the she-bear had hurt me then he would have had to sacrifice her, and he wasn't ready to carry the weight of another spirit on his back.

Do you carry many spirits around? Dani asked him.

Mistah smiled sweetly. He had grey eyes and very white, very beautiful teeth, apart from one gold tooth that projected its impure gleam from the back of his mouth.

It's not good to talk about the spirits that weigh us down, he said, lifting his shirt to show us the tattoos on his stomach. A snake coiled around his bellybutton and a puma stretched out across his ribcage.

I have more on my arms, too, Mistah said, and I remembered the thirst that was in Dani's voice when he'd told me about him.

As Mistah spoke, Dani explained the things I couldn't understand because his friend kept switching between languages. Dani understood almost everything. It could be said that he had mastered that language too, so much so that he'd even started translating for Aunt Anita. I interrupted the conversation with questions. Mistah was slow at telling his exaggerated stories, and I wanted to skip to the end, to find out which paths and situations in his human life had brought him all those animals, the ones he said he'd been forced to sacrifice, and not always to prevent a greater evil, but sometimes just to quell 'this fire', something he repeated again and again.

What else, what else? I asked. Mistah went quiet for a few seconds to catch his breath, then he continued to speak directly to Dani as if I didn't exist. He didn't look at me later, either, when he finally came out and said:

You have to learn to be more patient. You have to weave time better, you have to respect it. Patience and respect. How will you be able to live without dying?

That day I kept going over what Mistah had said. Live without dying. That hybrid language he spoke, Michif, was undeniably difficult, and I couldn't understand his real intentions, unlike Dani. One of the things I didn't know was when, exactly, on that afternoon full of frights and surprises, Mistah had got it into that big, beautiful head of Dani's that it was a good idea for us to leave. Mistah had laid out a simple plan for him: Dani, who had turned seventeen by then (not that that really mattered though, because those modern-day Amerindians still measured age in a different way) would marry Kenya, making him a Métis, not because the law said so (this Dani told me in the slow pattern of speech he copied from our friend) but because the bonds that really counted were formed above the canopies of the trees and on the high mountain peaks. Then we could cross over to the US without Aunt Anita or her consent, and our lives would be truly free.

It was clear that the proposal Mistah had drummed into my brother's head was now bursting into bloom with determination. The fresh intensity of that fixation was clogging up my brother's face without disfiguring it. Dani had made his mind up, and now I would have to choose which way to go.

I looked at Anne Escori again through the steamed-up window. There she was, fat and alcoholic, in that stinking hovel. When all was said and done, she was still our aunt, the sister Mamá had wanted to look after but who was now looking after us. Well, who was trying to look after us. Dani hadn't included Aunt Anita in our fate. And he hadn't asked me what I really wanted either. But what would I have told him if he had? Maybe my instinctive response would have been: 'For Mamá to be alive,' but of all the impossible things in this world, that was the most impossible. No doubt I would have been content with just asking for a chocolate ice cream or for hair like Kenya's, which was red because she used to grind up a seed and mix it with soil to use as dye. If Dani hadn't been gay, I'm sure he would have fallen deeply in love with Kenya, who was worthy of that secret nickname my brother had given her, Luna Sangrienta, because her hair seemed to catch fire in the setting sun. Luna Sangrienta, yes, even though she dressed like any other gringa in Winnipeg: in padded down coats and gumboots for walking in the snow and enduring the incredible winters and the false springs.

I felt around for a cent in my parka, but I never had any money on me.

I looked at the night sky. I remember it well. I can still see the clouds pushing forward, intent on covering the waning moon, biting into the little that remained of it. The wind dispersed the clouds and the moon remained intact, like a wedge of lemon. I closed my eyes and counted to ten. If, when I opened them, the moon was still clear, I would stay with Anne Escori in the house with the rotted beams. If the clouds had overpowered the moon, I would leave with Dani and his friend Mistah, and go wherever the truck loaded with thoroughbred horses took us. One, two, three, four, I began to count...

A week later, Dani said that the escape was going to need money. He had the good sense not to press me for the diamond, as I wouldn't have given it up for anything in the world. Carrying that jewel around made me feel safe. I held up the diamond and it lit up my face, and for a few seconds I felt like something inside of me was becoming more beautiful, despite how fat I'd grown and how dense the fuzz on my arms had become. I was nothing more than a downcast donkey, eternally surrounded by the grey aura of my fears. My pineal gland was already wreaking havoc on my physique. Much later I realised I could use this blubber to make my voice more powerful, to growl, to give praise, to cry singing.

In the weeks that followed, Mistah drove Dani to the hospitals and streetside first aid posts in his truck to sell his blood. The Métis never gave blood on the grounds of beliefs in their ancestors and silver threads coming fatally undone, so Dani's blood was highly prized. They collected almost five hundred dollars. I'm sure you can work out how much blood that was thirty-some years ago. Five hundred dollars was too much to spend on an overland journey to the US. It was enough to take them all the way to the end of the world. Aunt Anita was the only one to notice Dani turning pale, and so she promised to have us dewormed. She never did though. The same way she never took me to the doctor so they could analyse the difference between my pupils and discover that the malignant spirit had been climbing from the nape of my neck and was threatening to take over my body, fatally enthroned on my sella turcica.

The night of the Métis' annual buffalo hunt, Dani and I finally managed to get official permission from Aunt Anita to stay out late for the celebrations. By then, she had stopped threatening us with talk of the malignant spirit because we weren't children anymore and her stories of shadow people and demons no longer worked. Though, truth be told, the sight of our aunt's eternally swollen face was enough to make you believe that the whole realm she conjured to intimidate us – or at least me – really existed and hovered above her head. That night, we left her dinner out and laid her mattress in the middle of the living room floor because the rotten beams in her room looked so close to collapse. We lit the fire; Dani placed several logs upright to stop the flames dying out too quick. The mercury was going to dip, without a jot of consideration for humans and animals.

I hadn't told him my decision yet, but on our way to the settlement, Dani spoke to me as if everything were one long goodbye. He showed me the tattoo Mistah had drawn on his chest, mixing vegetable-based colours with the ashes of our parents. It was the infinity symbol, that number eight floating in the void, inside an eye. Dani confessed that he had helped himself to the money Aunt Anita kept in a Prince Albert tobacco tin; it wasn't much, but it would help, he said. I didn't like to think that Dani was driven by greed, but wasn't five hundred dollars enough to start a new life already? Why take the savings of an old soak as well? Dani read my mind and told me that if he wanted to start a business in the US, five hundred dollars was a paltry sum. Besides, Aunt Anita was bound to have other tins of money stashed away somewhere. He was willing to bet on it. He told me that maybe it was time for me to remember some of those kung fu chokeholds in case Anita and I ended up moving to Winnipeg and I had to go to school. I had forgotten all about the kung fu holds. Then again, a quick glance at my body, at the way my thighs chafed when I walked, was enough to conclude that I couldn't lift a leg any higher than the fresh spring grass and was hardly likely to take someone down with a martial arts move.

On the settlement, the Métis had pitched tents and the scent of grilled buffalo meat floated in the air like an intense provocation. Kenya was strumming a guitar and singing songs in Michif. She was wearing the hide of a donkey as a hood, ears and all. Her beautiful face, with its proud cheekbones, contrasted with the grey pelt that protected her from the cold.

That night we ate, drank and danced to the sound of violins like people possessed. Dani quickly felt light-headed, probably because constantly selling his blood had reduced the tolerance he'd always bragged about. When we used to compete against each other, taking little sips on the dregs of the bottles our aunt stowed away in the pantry, it was always Dani who won.

Feeling tired, I wanted to sit down beside Kenya, near the still-warm embers where the meat had been grilled. Kenya offered me her hood, and although I was scared of looking ridiculous and ugly beneath the ears of that animal hide, I didn't want to be rude so I put it on. Anyway, I looked for the best I had to offer, but all I could find was my voice. So I opened my big mouth and sang like never before. It was a gospel song I'd heard on the radio, a profound song of few words, which made my heart beat faster. It was the first gospel song I'd ever sung in my life.

Kenya said: You have the most dazzling voice I've ever heard, Donkey Skin.

I could feel myself blushing. I wanted to say, 'Thank you, Luna Sangrienta,' but I held back because I didn't want the slightest misunderstanding to tarnish our friendship. I also thought I didn't look half bad under that furry hood; not only did it hide my blubber, it also brought me closer to that mysterious, natural way of life of the inhabitants of that settlement. It was a shame Dani wanted to leave the place where we finally felt at home.

After midnight, when most of the men were three sheets to the wind and some of the women were cackling in a wilder, more lustful way than before, Mistah asked Dani to go to the barn with him. One of the old men said something in Michif and gave a wicked laugh.

Half an hour must have passed when Kenya asked me if I wanted to go with her to see the horses that had been earmarked for the big equestrian competition in Minnesota. We could brush their manes or trim their dry ends to make them look like what they really were, princes of the prairies, masters of speed and wind. They're our representatives, Kenya said.

Don't be gone too long! one of the Métis men shouted out, the same old guy who had been joking with Mistah and Dani. His face, shrouded in bitter tobacco smoke, expressed not a single concern. It was the face of a man who calmly recognises the extremes of the world: rain or hell. Boredom or the resurrection of loved ones. His glassy, pale-blue eyes were exactly the same as Aunt Anita's. Perhaps in past lives they too had been brother and sister. But this was another life.

Make sure you get back before these bonfires go out. There are white folks hanging around, don't go pulling any tricks, the old man laughed again.

My happiness was sealed; Dani and I weren't thought of as white folks on the settlement. We were like any other relative there. For a second, the image of Aunt Anita sleeping spreadeagled on the mattress we'd left in the middle of the room troubled me. She, indeed, would be a drunk white woman at the annual buffalo festival.

Neither Kenya nor I were shocked to hear Mistah and Dani panting in one of the stalls. We didn't pretend it was coming from the animals, and we didn't cough or interrupt like people do sometimes when they're feeling awkward. Something inside of me was happy for Dani. Forgive me, Preacher Jeremy. There was this inexplicable tingling sensation burning inside my belly. My brother's frantic voice, his groans, the husky words Petite Mort whispered to him, were all part of a special act that I couldn't understand. But I wasn't there to understand. My fate had guided me there. The Lord's fate, Preacher Jeremy, dear doctors, brothers and sisters of the Niagara Church.

Kenya was smiling. She had pulled out a bone-handled switchblade and had started snipping gently at a pony's mane. It was very beautiful, that pony. Everything was beautiful that night.

Everything was beautiful until the headlamps of a Jeep lit up the back door of the barn, near the troughs. Kenya yelled something, Mistah! Mistah! she said, in an anxious tone completely alien to the characteristic calm of the Métis.

The white guys who climbed out of the Jeep weren't armed, which I took as a sign of hope or thought might stand in our favour. They were five big men with long hair styles that were fashionable back then, the kind some pop singers had. Only one of them was carrying a long metal rod, a tool for trucks. I blinked three times to make sure it wasn't just a scene that my faithful companion, fear, had projected into the gloom of the barn. When I opened my eyes, they were still there.

They shone a torch on Mistah's face; he'd barely had time to pull up his trousers, while the biggest of them had grabbed my brother from behind, in a hold that was clearly immune to any of the kung fu moves we might remember from our childhood prehistory.

Those men in the barn claimed that Mistah owed them money from bets and heroin. They searched through pockets, inside boots, they hit all of us. I thought I was going to spit out my cavity-ridden teeth.

Where the hell is our money? Did you think our grade-A China White was an offering from your stupid gods? It's time to pay, bitch!

They were calling Mistah a bitch.

I really felt like I was going to throw up... I... I don't want to go into more detail, Preacher Jeremy, because I think by now we've all understood what happened at the annual buffalo festival. Those men sodomised Mistah, and while they did, Dani wept like he'd never wept before, not even at our parents' absolute death. The men were pulling back my brother's hair, making sure he didn't miss a single second of that horror show. One of them, a man wearing lipstick and fishnet stockings, got really close to Kenya's round face and spoke to her with the falsest sweetness:

I have two options for our princess here. Shave her. Leave her hide nice and smooth, so that everyone knows she and her ancestors owe a shit ton of money. Or slice her up.

Kenya didn't have time to choose between those two 'options'. In a matter of seconds, the guy snatched the knife from the beautiful Luna Sangrienta and tore a slit along the left side of her face, almost to her ear.

There was black blood on the pastures. There was blood. A lot. There were, perhaps, spine-chilling rivers of blood treacherously fertilising the crop fields, invisible, sticky blades of grass that soiled everything: air and breath, wood and metal. There was blood, the kind that sticks to the soles of your shoes, making your footsteps devour your heels with their betrayal.

I thought I was going to die that night. Listening to Dani crying, listening to those men's beastly groans and to Kenya's whimpers becoming more and more muffled, I couldn't imagine my own punishment.

But... Punishment for what? Punishment for what? a voice inside of me began to ask. Punishment for what? that voice began to yell. And so I yelled with a power I didn't recognise, I yelled with all the fat on my body, I yelled from my pineal gland, I know that now. I roared so hard that those men were surely shocked to hear a sound like that coming from me, from my nauseated throat. So hard, that even I could barely tell that it wasn't me roaring but the she-bear, the same bear Mistah had stopped before she could annihilate me with a swipe of the claw. It was the she-bear now, cornering three of those guys in the last stall and roaring with a pain that could only stem from the spirit, and from humiliation, and from wounded love.

I don't know if the worst thing of all happened at daybreak. As I told you before, this growth inside my brain, which is trying to dominate the sella turcica of my pituitary gland and surround the pineal butterfly with its venom, prevents me from putting each link in the right order. Time and respect, Mistah once said. I've respected these memories that I'm sharing with you today as I bear witness, in case the operation wrenches them from me and all that remains in my skull is a void. No more imagination. The doctors say that the operation will be only minimally invasive, much less so than expected, and for that I can thank the gospel, my she-bear exhalations, the concave fervour of the roof of my mouth, this cure full of love. The pineal gland, they say, is fuelled by air and frequencies and hormone levels. Gospel music is all of these things.

Dani and I walked home in silence. It was impossible to talk, breathe, understand or speak. We walked, propelled by force of habit. Dani smelled of shit – his or Mistah's – and horse dung. From time to time he sobbed. The Métis had forbidden us from calling the police. This unforgivable offence had happened on their territory and they would know how best to deliver justice. A few miles away we noticed a warm glow, which gave the forest a different aura. It was me who started running. Dani followed me instinctively, with the obedience of a zombie.

Our house was a monumental burning bush lapping at the tree trunks and advancing through the back garden like a legion. I knew that that almighty crackle was the sound of all the skeletons that had tormented me. The bones of the birch trees, our parents' skulls, and now Aunt Anita's too.

The authorities were likely to spend a few days trying to identify our remains among the debris from the fire, days that would give us a head start. We weren't bolting, I assure you. This was just another pirouette on the long journey we'd set out on when Aunt Anita signed the custody documents. Dani said it would be best if we split up, because the Métis had warned him that the men who'd humiliated Mistah were out looking for him.

You can have the diamond, I said to Dani, with an unknown strength.

Dani looked at the jewel fondly, then he smiled and slipped it into his pocket. Years later I saw a rock just like it. It was a stalactite.

It was also years before I found out that Dani was murdered. Different guys though. By that point, Dani was using an indigenous name and his death, his little death, was the result of a drunken brawl.

In the end, my journey was the longest. My brothers and sisters of the Niagara Church, you know how many minor falls the Lord sowed along my path. When I got too big to keep drifting from one foster home to the next, I crossed over to the US. I sang in bars, I filled up my heart with cocaine, and I must confess that it wasn't half bad. Perhaps my personality contains particles of the same vital impulse that pushed my aunt towards the fascinating cliff-edge that the self can be – that profound quest, dangerous knowledge. If I decided to follow the precepts of the Niagara Church, it was because they gave me what my whole being needed: to sing, to roar, to use my she-bear voice to shatter the air. Forgive me, Preacher Jeremy, that's just how it is.

You see, it was the incredible singers of the Niagara Church that taught me the gospel technique. From day one, they explained that my talent didn't depend on those techniques, but on my heart. They also said that my voice wounded and healed, that it was a deep, dazzling voice. That's what they said, and that's what I understood.

I've shared this long testimony with you all today, before my operation, and in case the laser incinerates my memory, to thank you for the years of gospel music. The first thing this generous song taught me was to breathe, to turn oxygen into nourishment. And that breath was where the Lord worked his miracle. The doctors say that by inhaling with my stomach and exhaling into those songs of praise, I was able to systematically inhibit the growth of the malignant mass and protect the incredibly delicate area that surrounds the pineal gland. If not, I would have died years ago, without the chance to show you who I am today, the person I mightn't have become if my parents hadn't died in the Yungas, or if my aunt hadn't sought the oblivion of alcohol because she was weighed down by all those memories of Paris, or if I hadn't walked beside Dani to the annual buffalo festival. Thanks to gospel music, I experienced the ecstasy, 'the major lift' that Leonard Cohen celebrates in his beautiful hymn. Thanks to gospel music, I discovered that I carry the spirit of that she-bear in my brain, right here between my two hemispheres; it's the she-bear who sings and who roars when I stand up and project my voice. It's Ayotchow the bear, not me. Forgive me, Preacher Jeremy, forgive me, brothers and sisters. It's the she-bear. It's Ayotchow. Remember this when you're writing up my medical case for the science journal that wanted it. Remember, please, that my real name is Ayotchow, the she-bear of the gospel.

KINDRED DEER

The medicinal smell that rises from Joaquín's body like an aura has taken over our bedroom. It'll be gone in a few days, they told him. But this time it's different. Eight blood samples a day, bland diet, zero sun exposure. The pay's good, that's for sure. We won't have to worry about the rent for a few months. Joaquín will have no regrets as he writes his thesis on the cloning of Andean llamas and other species of camelids, and I'll try to publish mine, an overly structured investigation of 'The Realm of Magic Realism', as I pretentiously called it at the time, though it bores me now. And of course, I'll have hours to devote to making sense of my brother's birth chart. When it comes to the cosmos, I'm at best an illiterate fool stammering out a system of symbols I barely understand.

You should apply for a research grant, I tell him. That way we can turn the page on this whole medical trial business. I don't like what we're doing, Joa. What they're doing to you. You say this is the safest stage, that they wouldn't be doing it on humans if it wasn't. But I have my doubts, you know? They couldn't care less about who they use as 'subjects' – or what was it you said they call you again?

Prospective subjects, Joaquín says, in that gravelly voice he's been left with by the people at the hospital.

Prospective subjects?

Yes, that's it.

Well, whatever. Monkeys, subjects, people – it's all the same to them. What do I know.

I run my hand over his ribs, because that's what my fingers touch beneath his parched skin. The excess of vitamin A has obliterated his epidermis. He still can't expose it to the sun. I remember this, and I'm not exactly convinced by the black muslin curtains I found among the remnants of Halloween products in the Walmart sale. A glare dimmed by the gothic voile, but persistent and harmful nonetheless, covers us.

What happens if you get a lot of daylight? Will you turn into a vampire or something?

I've explained this to you already. My liver. It could trigger toxic hepatitis. There was a case like that in the last trial. The lawsuit cost them a fortune; that's why we have to sign clause 27 now. No lawsuits. No sun. No children.

We'd spawn little monsters.

Exactly.

Well, nothing we can't produce without the help of this trial... What did you say it was called again?

Counteractive A. It's a provisional name. If the results are good, I'm sure they'll come up with a proper pharma-ceutical name for it, the kind that can kill any virus just by being said out loud.

Counteractive A – sounds like a military operation. And when can we fuck again?

Right now if you want. With a rubber, of course.

I hate condoms. When can we fuck without one?

In six months, amor mío. When there's no trace of this substance left in my body. Also, when you agree to take those antihistamines for contraceptive allergies. They give them to us for free at the medical trial. Or do you like the idea of having a child with two heads?

Talk about complicated: antihistamines for contraceptive allergies. Barrier against barrier. Give me abstinence any day!

I don't know how long we spent sleeping beneath that black-tinted glare. Joaquín on his side, sweating out the residue of the latest-generation concoction that promises to cure all ills, his neck limp like a chicken ready to be turned into food. Me trying to use my body to protect Joaquín's Christ-like back, that dehydrated canvas unspoiled by so much as a birthmark, only the suggestion of his shoulder blades, undeniable proof of the divine refusal to turn us into better creatures, into fallen angels or birds of an ordinary but happy species. All these things I think of when I look at Joaquín's back. Or rather, I always think behind my husband's back. We could have sprawled out to watch YouTube videos on the living room rug, but we haven't vacuumed in weeks and the threadbare fibres are still covered in the particles of all the pets we were looking after for a few dollars on the side until recently. We even took in injured birds that worked at strengthening the muscles in their wings with short flights between the highest beams of the cottage. And geckos that got by just fine on their own. Feathers, hairs, tiny scales all over the place. And that fine dust, which blows over from the hills of Ithaca at the end of autumn, as if they were the ones shedding and not us. Hair, dust, and the scent of chemicals, of ludicrous mixtures that humiliate the liver. Both of us defeated by a despondency the money ought to make disappear but strangely only serves to highlight. Both of us defeated...

I wake up to the sound of the shower. I also hear, muffled by the water, Joaquín's cough. The glare through the window is now a clear night. The kind of night that comes before snow. I sit up and spy the silhouettes of three deer crossing the field. They must be the same ones that come back each day to cover up the dead heap we're too bone idle to report to the animal office or whatever that place is called. Anyway, when the snow is unleashed, it will eventually bury our friend the deer and everyone else in peace. Then I slowly remember that I've dreamed of the possible child Joaquín and I would have under the influence of Counteractive A, a child made from vitamins and money we don't know how to use. It floated inside me like a creature from the deep yonder. Facing the mirror, with a six-month belly, I could make out each part of its unborn flesh through the translucent skin of my stomach: the two heads, the eyelids closed beneath the soft foetal oedema, the perfect little hands and the little feet crowned with supernumerary toes; those tiny, primitive feet that someone had sewn together at the heels, forming petals abounding in newly formed tissue. Tiny son in bloom that throbbed inside my belly. Or would it be a daughter? If only my recollection were revealing a tiny vulva in this spotty remembering of the dream. I move closer to the window and press my nose against the freezing cold glass. I wipe away the condensation that clings to it, created by the contrast between the air in the room and the temperature outside. A stag walks over as though he has recognised me, just as I recognise him; it's the same one that visited his kin a few days ago. He has one antler longer than the other.

Hello.

The stag kicks out three times. It must be some kind of greeting. Then another comes up, probably one of its young. I don't know what they call baby deer – deer cubs, perhaps? This language of ours is too deficient to venture into that world of elegance and beauty. The stag pushes the younger deer with two head butts, off you go, get back to grieving the dead heap. The deer are so close to my window that I can see the melancholy of their eyelashes. If it were up to me, I would make sure my Counteractive A child had the beautiful, straight eyelashes of a deer.

Off you trot, go with your kid, I tell the stag. And he does as I say.

In the morning I crack an egg, just for me. Lecithin is fatal for Joaquín's congested liver. I focus on the egg, occasionally glancing at the arthritic tree through the kitchen window. Until just a few days ago that tree was a burning flame, a profuse bundle of crimson leaves. But not today, poor thing. That window won't let any sunlight in. The sun always greets us through the living room. Even now, with the sheet of black muslin outlawing the day, the cold sun is still doing its utmost to burn objects. In astrology, when a planet gets too close to the sun, it loses its personality; stunned by the brilliance of that giant star, the smaller planet goes blind. My brother was a Scorpio, with Venus and Neptune in that same house, too. The planets of love and ideals got so close to his Sun that they combusted in the searing heat and couldn't tilt and project outwards; they couldn't break through to life to defend my brother's soul from the violence that others always pose. Quite the opposite: Neptune and Venus, maddened by the great light, returned furious to my brother's anarchic heart and stabbed it, shredding all hope, confidence, trust, the flicker of his own image, the slightest possibility of redemption.

141

With my left hand, I struggle to flip the egg and it turns out like a blister, neat but uneven at the edges. I flip it anyway, and the oil hisses at my chest. I wet my index finger with spit and rub the spot where the oil stings. I try not to use my right arm while I'm at home, it's my tool for working at the supermarket. Sometimes I try to emotionally detach myself from my arm. I think of it as an orthopaedic gripper, a tool that grabs objects – shampoo, meat, razors, cereals, mesh bags of organic fruit, adhesive for false teeth – and slides them from left to right with the light touch of someone with mechanical springs for muscles. I've tried to slide objects with my left hand, but when I do so I can no longer position the codes against the reader with the correct precision. I end up doing the job twice, the height of stupidity. Once again, I instruct my arm to behave in a cyborg-like manner, we don't want the self-service checkouts to take this miserable part-time job away from us. And so this egg is bound to break on me, as if it had been punched in its little golden face.

I make myself a piece of toast too, and I glaze it with honey. Joaquín gets a portion of poached chicken and a cup of coffee for his breakfast, lucky him.

It's definitely going to snow today, says Joaquín.

Let's hope so. That way we won't have to call the animal office.

How many days has it been now? he asks, swallowing saliva. His throat must be dry too. Shame he can't eat yoghurt either.

I go over to the window and draw the black curtain slightly, as if the sight of the dead heap were going to give me the right answer.

It must be four days now. No, no, five. It's been there since Friday. You got back from the medical trial on Sunday. That's right, it's been five days.

It smells awful now. Don't you think?

I wouldn't say awful. It smells, yes, but no worse than that bin in the garage, the one the rats have already rifled through. It'll snow soon, and that'll be the cure-all. No more smell, no more dead heap. It'll be gone and buried like Atlantis.

Why don't we just call the people at the animal office and let them take care of it?

You call them. My English isn't great and I hate it when they pass me from operator to operator like a thousand times. Anyway, I have to dash. I'm only doing three hours of customer service today, so I have to go in with extra supplies of good mood.

I'll do it after lunch, when you get back. I'm sure they don't get as many reports in the afternoons.

After lunch, however, I discover the mark on Joaquín's back, that fakir's back, which until the night before had been an immaculate sheet.

What's that?

I hold up the Moroccan mirror from the hall and he inspects his reflection, which bounces back in the magical little magnifying mirror I use to ferociously pluck out my eyebrows. It's not a big blotch; it's more like a subtle fingerprint, or as if someone (not me) had sunk their thumb into him in the glorious moments of orgasm.

Did you bang yourself on something?

No, not that I recall. But with the side-effects and all...

Shouldn't you report it?

Let's wait a while. I don't want to go all the way there and be made to fill out forms or have my blood taken again.

I wonder what they do with all that blood they take from you?

Just analyse it, that's all, store it. They keep it as a record, as evidence, scientific proof. How else are they going to defend themselves against the WHO or complaints from some anti-pharma hippy or other? With our blood, of course!

Joaquín's strong reaction takes me by surprise, especially because now, as the premature night sets in again, he looks even paler than he did this morning. It's a fervent reaction that resembles fury. Perhaps that's the point of clinical trials, to synthesise the hybris of all the emotions – indignation and fear, for example – and see whether that unbearable contradiction makes us edge further away from the places where we, anaesthetised, harbour unspeakable ambitions. 'Fervofuria': that's the kind of creative name they should give the drug that's currently transforming my husband. He's right though; his blood is what they want. They need it to protect themselves from any potential mishaps. Blood converted into code, statistics and trends. Nothing more irrefutable than mathematical blood. Scientific plasma that will allow them to market that prodigious formula designed to fight leprosy, acne, AIDS, the sorrows of the soul, and all the infectious diseases that have cropped up in the era of climate change. For some reason, this all reminds me of a case I studied for my thesis. The story of Azucena de Quito, a young woman who achieved sainthood by the only means permitted for such lofty ambitions: tormenting herself. This sickly girl from the seventeenth century had her blood drained daily. Catalina, the indigenous servant tasked with disposing of the extractions that the bloodletter took every day at noon, poured the liquid into a flowerpot in the garden. And in that fertilised soil, the most beautiful white lily grew, a flower that never wilted, that closed up at night and opened at dawn, always anew, in complete possession of time. From that lily came a scent that stirred the soul. How many journeys must the servant girl Catalina have soared on, sweetly enraptured by the perfume of that blood?

Joaquín's blood performs miracles too. We were poor before, but not now. We were on the verge of declaring bankruptcy, but not anymore. We were worried sick and having sleepless nights about our debts, but now our credit rating is safe. We will live like this, from medical trial to medical trial, until Joaquín himself becomes a doctor full of futuristic answers or I find a position with some semblance of dignity in a humanities department, allowing me to finally leave my part-time job as a cashier in Walmart. *Did you find everything okay? Have a nice day! And, of course, Merry Christmas and Happy holidays!*

I venture into the mist with my poncho for protection. I turn on my smartphone flashlight and tiptoe towards the dead heap. The virgin snow is still like cotton wool, but I continue to tread carefully because I know there's no other way to enter the realm of the night; too trusting, and the ground can open up and you'll find yourself somewhere else. Yelling wouldn't save me from that subterranean abduction. Living so far away from everything, surrounded by the Finger Lakes and the rumbling waterfalls, my cry would surely be confused for the howl of some wolf beset by hunger.

The deer's eyes are open and there is still a glimmer in those corneas. It must be an effect of the cold materialising on all the surfaces. It's true: the deer reeks, a stench between bitterness and sweetness that isn't yet unbearable but infuses the air in short bursts. And it's true that its belly, sliced open by a gunshot, has been fodder for the local rats; they've devoured its guts, maggots and all. I saw them there, digging with that sinister air rodents have when they eat: diligent, meticulous. Maybe they even camped out there for the first few days, seeking the last vestiges of warmth. We all have to survive the damned winter – truth be told, I don't blame them.

I crouch down to get a better look at the carcass. I run the flashlight over it, unable to escape the very sad feeling that I'm hurting something invisible. It's a doe: no antlers. On her tattered belly I can still see her teats; they're swollen, either due to the violent way she died or because she was pregnant, I'm not sure which. If there was a baby, the rats would have eaten it. A profound, uncomfortable urge to cry comes over me. I reach out to stroke the deer's haunches.

What in God's name are you doing?

I fall flat on my backside. A wave of nausea hits me.

Shit! Nothing. What are you doing outside?

The moon won't kill me.

But the cold will. They told you to be careful not to get sick. You really have to leave that fucked-up experiment.

Holy shit, that beast stinks!

Don't say that, please…. Don't call her a beast.

The seventh day after the medical trial, we decide to go to the hospital. The blotch on Joaquín's skin has spread and now covers a large area of his back, like a vast body of water nibbling away at the sand with serene passion. The snow has been falling non-stop, so we drive at a moderate speed, taking extra care with these tyres, which have been patched up repeatedly and haven't been changed for three years. We promised we'd eventually get round to buying proper tyres for the snow, the kind with little teeth, but they're so expensive that we keep talking each other out of it, reminding ourselves that the snow will stop eventually. We also had to wait until nightfall before we set off on this long journey; Joaquín mustn't be exposed to even a speck of that poisonous light multiplied by the white landscape. He searches for a Bolivian radio station on his phone and connects it to the Bluetooth. Those voices, those beloved accents arrive muffled by the interference from the bad weather. 'They're killing us,' someone sobs in an interview. I fidget in my seat. I want to know more about the desperate 'us' that reveals itself in that broken voice.

My mom says it's like a different country, Joaquín tells me. Maybe we should go, see for ourselves how they're doing.

My sister says people have changed so much that they're not the same any more. I don't know if we should go, Joa. Not now. Let's get ourselves out of debt first.

We're not the same any more either, are we? Joaquín tries to joke, glancing at himself in the rear-view mirror. The peanut butter balm on his chapped lips doesn't seem to offer any kind of relief; the incurable crusts are still there, straining the corners of his mouth into an almost cynical expression.

We drive past the farms in the area; the dark wooden barns that loom like temples of satanic religions always make me picture kidnapped girls who have forgotten their names, young women restrained by chains as thick as the ones that tank-treaded snow ploughs use to push through these white swamps, so I close my eyes and only open them when I figure that we've made it to a prettier stretch of road. That's the military cemetery, over there. 'The final resting place of our heroes,' a sign on the path at the entrance timidly announces. I suppose as far as this culture of medals and nationalism is concerned, going to

147

war is enough to turn you into a hero, and even more so if you return home ground to dust in a sealed casket decorated with the colours of the flag. I've never ventured into those grounds sown with crosses, but not for lack of wanting. What attracts me – besides the tragic beauty of the graves, of that final, almost haughty indifference with which they stand there – is the summarised story of each life. Let's suppose a soldier was born on 5 April 1995 and had to join the army in 2013, during one of the worst quadratures of Saturn and Pluto (probably obeying the instinct of an impulsive personality incapable of finding peace in contemplation) and his body was blown up by a grenade that same year, when Uranus was giving his birth moon a terrible aspect. What I would calculate with the code of the stars is this: the imprint of that soldier's fate, its subtlest equation, the point where the soul begins and the way it arches towards its end, that hypnotised descent to the eighth house. Everything else – the disappointments and love, or the addiction to those drugs of war that surely required prospective subjects like Joaquín, the dark jokes, the nightmares or sudden desires, all the things that give form to ghosts – all of that I leave well alone. My knowledge doesn't extend that far. The 'theory of the stars', as Ptolemy says, would take up my whole existence. May the heroes rest in peace.

In the hospital, sure enough, Joaquín has to fill out a lot of forms. But at least we don't have to wait like everyone else. If this were a hotel or an airport, or even the waiting room of purgatory, they would say we were VIPs. The hospital staff usher us straight through to the labs on the prospective subjects ward, where we arrive exhausted after traipsing through corridors, gardens, lifts, little manmade groves, then more corridors and wide doorways. Although Joaquín says he doesn't mind sitting or standing, they insist he lies down on a sterile stretcher

– we can tell that's what it is because they've taken off a plastic sheet that was covering its whole surface – and they make me wear a surgical mask. The view from the room is beautiful, the window looks out onto a narrow strip of Cayuga Lake. Beams shimmer on the water from the lighthouses. Joaquín and I are captivated by the scene of a man fishing with infinite patience. Night fisherman are common in this corner of the world.

Two doctors appear, and Joaquín greets them as if they were cousins or old friends from his PhD. The doctors, though, don't even remove their gloves or surgical masks to shake my husband's hand. One of them speaks in English, the other tries his hand at Spanish.

So, how's that thesis coming along? We want you with us on the team soon.

They greet me too and ask me to wait outside, in a friendly tone that smacks of guilt.

I tell them – I'm not sure how disdainfully – that I'd rather stay.

They have the decency to acquiesce.

When all is said and done, Joaquín is the other half of me. At this very moment, inside my own body, in my kidneys, I can feel the searing heat of my cells empathising with every sensation as they puncture his back, completely taken over by that irrational bruise.

Are you sure it wasn't an accident?

No, no.

Are you completely sure?

Well, no, not sure… I can't be sure. Anything and everything cuts my skin. It's like my blood's ready and waiting to clot. In Bolivia we call these bruises 'moretes', Joaquín smiles, his eyes meeting mine. I smile back at him from under the pointless mask.

In a case of hypovolemic hypersensitivity, the slightest graze can trigger…

149

Ecchymosis. Of course, that's one possibility.

But it's not serious. Say it out loud so my wife won't worry.

The doctors say nothing. They just keep the tubes of Joaquín's black blood and tell me they'll be back with clinical tests.

Joaquín and I find ourselves alone again. I go over to the window, seeking the tranquillity of Cayuga Lake.

They'll have to pay me extra for this, surely, he says.

I study his face to see whether he's joking. He isn't. But there's a desperate glint or look in his eyes, something in the way he raises his eyebrows.

Pay you extra?

Yes. Clause 27, plus an acknowledgement of non-maleficence, which is a questionable principle whichever way you look at it. I've done everything they asked me to. And that's exactly why I'm the most desirable subject now.

You don't say? I hear my voice turning shrill out of impotence. I stroke the roof of my mouth with my tongue, it calms me down.

Yes. Just wait until they get back, then you'll see.

But it takes the doctors a couple of hours to reappear. During the wait, Joaquín and I have decided that when we get out of this, we're going to use the cure-all money they give us to buy tickets to Bolivia. It doesn't matter if everything has changed there; it doesn't matter if, as my sister says, our friends have become distant and there's bewilderment and rage hanging over every conversation. We'll go anyway.

We need to do more tests, they explain. You'll have to stay in here for a few days, but of course those days will be covered by the money you're getting from the trial.

The same rate of pay as the first phase?

Same conditions.

In that case, no.

What do you mean, no? The doctor instinctively makes to pull off his surgical mask but stops himself.

You should be paying me twice that. Otherwise I'll look for hospital care on my own.

Both doctors turn to face me, probably hoping I'll make Joaquín see sense. I let my gaze wander back over to my husband; I see a man full of intelligence, of scientific ambitions, a man at the mercy of the churned-up blood that has started climbing his neck, staining the skin purple atop his first vertebra. Wayward blood that will do God knows what when it has finished covering his skull.

Pay him double or we're leaving, I say. I could add: And we'll take Joaquín's body to the highest bidder. But a night as absurd as this is hardly the time for another outburst.

Joaquín signs plenty more documents, and they make me sign one too, promising I'll let the research team keep my husband's body if he dies during Phase X. They'll pay me a hefty sum if that happens. There are almost no subjects in Phase X. This phase no longer has a number. It belongs in the same category as the cases from that series, *The X Files*.

To say goodbye to Joaquín, they make me put on a hazmat suit. It has nothing on those outfits astronauts wear when they launch themselves into space, happily blinded by the Sagittarian ambition of travellers, full of the kind of emboldened jubilation that only Aries in its first degrees can give to the native. I walk forwards in my suit and I hug Joaquín, who is now dressed in one of those humiliating hospital gowns. I feel his muscles and the closeness of his skeleton as if in the fog of a dream.

If I die, rescue me, my husband says, his eyes wet.

I press him against my sterile coveralls, and I know I should give him my word:

I swear. If you die, I'll come for you.

I get back to the cottage at dawn. I tear the stupid muslin from the living room window and stuff it in my mouth. I don't know what makes me do this. It must be because I want to punish my Neptunian blindness, my inability to offer Joaquín good advice. Everything looked so promising with that favourable Jupiter aspecting his ascendent. Didn't I know that Jupiter is also overindulgence, inflammation, excess, short-lived glory, flooding, insatiable lust, roaring laughter and splendour, the spontaneous star, the cosmic feast? Is it not, perhaps, the first mirage of death?

I go out to the field and quicken my step, on the run from myself, making for the dead heap.

There it is. There she is. She hasn't left me alone.

I brush the snow from her haunches and cover her with the sheet of muslin. Her gaping body no longer shelters maggots. It's almost a cave that I could fit into myself.

I get down on my knees, I try to pray but the words won't come out. I don't remember. I'm overcome with other things. Then, little by little, Ptolemy's words come to me. Listen to this, deer. It's for you:

'I know that I am mortal, the creature of one day. But when I explore the winding courses of the stars I no longer touch with my feet the earth. I am standing near Zeus himself, drinking my fill of Ambrosia, the food of the gods.'

I repeat the words over and over, so that the snow, so deaf and methodical, listens too, so that the waterfalls listen, so that my voice shatters the Finger Lakes, so that the orphaned deer come, so that the hunters and the doctors can hear me, so that the arthritic trees quiver, so that the guilt and the rage do not drown me.

ACKNOWLEDGEMENTS

I would like to thank Alexander Torres, Denis Fernández, Magela Baudoin, Betina González, Liliana Colanzi, Sebastián Antezana, Keiko Oyakawa, Anabel Gutiérrez, Gladys Varona-Lacey, Alejandra Hornos, Claudia Bowles, Herlinda Flores, María Gavidia, Alex Quintanilla, Luis Miguel Rivas Granada and Freddy Arana, for their feedback, for their faith in the first breath of these characters.

And my parents.

TRANSLATOR'S REFERENCES

Bataille, Georges. *The Collected Poems of Georges Bataille,* tr. M. Spitzer (Wyomissing, PA: Dufour Editions, 1999).

Blyth, R.H. *Haiku, Vol. 2: Spring* (Tokyo: Hokuseido, 1950).

Edmonds, Radcliffe G., *Drawing Down the Moon: Magic in the Ancient Greco-Roman World* (Princeton, NJ: Princeton University Press, 2019), p. 260.

Hoffmann, Yoel (ed.) *Japanese Death Poems: Written by Zen Monks and Haiku Poets on the Verge of Death* (Clarendon, VT: Tuttle Publishing, 1998), p. 64.

Musashi, Miyamoto. *The Book of Five Rings*, tr. William Scott Wilson (Boulder, CO: Shambhala, 2012), p. 108.

CHARCO PRESS

Director & Editor: Carolina Orloff
Director: Samuel McDowell

www.charcopress.com

Fresh Dirt from the Grave was published on
80gsm Munken Premium Cream paper.

The text was designed using Bembo 11.5 and ITC Galliard.

Printed in January 2023 by TJ Books
Padstow, Cornwall, PL28 8RW using responsibly
sourced paper and environmentally-friendly adhesive.